Praise for Shelli Stevens's
Seducing Allie

"The story is well written and the reader won't want to put this down until it's finished. I definitely want to find more stories written by this delightful author."

~ *The Romance Studio*

"This is a nice, easy read. It is just the thing to bring to the beach (or camping!) and while away an hour or two."

~ *Long and Short Reviews*

Look for these titles by
Shelli Stevens

Now Available:

Seducing Allie

Shelli Stevens

SAMHAIN
PUBLISHING

Samhain Publishing, Ltd.
11821 Mason Montgomery Road, 4B
Cincinnati, OH 45249
www.samhainpublishing.com

Seducing Allie
Copyright © 2011 by Shelli Stevens
Print ISBN: 978-1-60928-610-1
Digital ISBN: 978-1-60928-500-5

Editing by Tera Kleinfelter
Cover by Scott Carpenter

This book is a work of fiction. The names, characters, places, and incidents are products of the writer's imagination or have been used fictitiously and are not to be construed as real. Any resemblance to persons, living or dead, actual events, locale or organizations is entirely coincidental.

First Samhain Publishing, Ltd. electronic publication: July 2011
First Samhain Publishing, Ltd. print publication: June 2012

Dedication

Thank you to my editor, Tera. To my family, friends, and readers for their wonderful support.

Chapter One

"Did you see the paper this morning?"

"Paper?" Allison muttered absently, her attention focused on her toenails currently being painted. *Maybe that red was too orange.* "I don't really read the paper."

It was the last Friday of the month, and Allison had been looking forward to her monthly breakfast, pedicure and gossip session with her best friend. And after the fatteningly awesome meal they'd just had, sitting in a pedicure chair and letting her stomach settle was pretty much heaven.

She just needed to make it to another step class this weekend to burn off that damn biscuits and gravy from Voula's.

"Does that red look too orange?" Allison voiced her worries aloud, her brows drawing together.

Leah leaned forward in her chair to look at Allison's feet. "No, it looks good. You can totally pull it off. But then you could paint your nails with mud and pull it off, you sexy thing."

Mud... A memory flickered through Allison's head and her lips curved into a small smile. Her and Clint Novak, running barefoot through a muddy field during the summer, chasing after butterflies.

God, that was a long time ago. She'd grown up since then, changing into a woman who wouldn't be caught dead ruining a pedicure in the mud. And Clint...well, he'd stayed a little more true to his childhood habits. A forest ranger in Montana. When was the last time she'd seen him? A year ago? Had it really been that long?

"Why did you ask about the paper?"

"Oh. Well, I'm sure you've already heard," Leah cleared her throat. "But, uh, there was an article about Kenneth's engagement."

Allison just barely avoided choking on the cough drop she'd been sucking on. "Kenneth's getting *married?*"

All thoughts of Clint evaporated as her focus turned to his childhood best friend. The man she'd dated last year for a few months. "But...why didn't he tell me?"

"Who knows with that guy."

Allison's stomach sank and her newly done nails bit into the fake leather handles on the chair. It wasn't possible. It just couldn't be true. They were friends. They'd all been friends— her, Clint and Kenneth. Until Clint had stopped coming around or calling a year ago. Right around when she and Kenneth had started dating, really. And recently Kenneth had pretty much cut her out of his life too.

"Since you didn't know, you obviously aren't aware of the really bad part."

"There's a really bad part?" She held her breath, eyes widening as she glanced at Leah again.

Leah's face crinkled into a wince. "He's marrying Ashley Phelps."

"Bullshit! That little gold-digging whore? I heard he was sleeping with her, but *marrying* her?"

"You swear way too much for a second grade teacher," Leah said with a sigh and flipped the page in her magazine.

"Did she get knocked up?"

"Allison!"

"Seriously, she once told me in vivid detail how someone could fake a pregnancy. That girl is bad news."

"Yikes, that is bad. But who knows if that's what happened. Anyway, it's his life," Leah reminded her gently. "Kenneth's a big boy now."

Allison stared down at the woman doing her nails—who was chatting quietly with the woman doing Leah's toes—but didn't really see her. Her thoughts were flying a mile a minute.

Kenneth was a friend. A good one. So maybe he'd started being a jerk lately—well, since he'd started sleeping with Ashley, apparently—but did he really know what he was getting into marrying this girl? Ashley had never made it a secret she planned to marry for money, and Kenneth had plenty of it. Or his family did...

"Hey, forget about Kenneth. I probably shouldn't have even said anything." Leah sighed. "Besides, you know you're going to meet him."

"Meet who?"

"The man who's going to rock your world and make you forgot your own name."

Allison's lips quirked. "He's going to give me amnesia?"

"*Allison.*"

"What? Look, we're not even talking about *my* dating habits." Allison shook her head and sighed, tired of this same old conversation. "But since you brought it up, let me just say I'll be twenty-five in two months and I'm tired of it. I'm swearing off dating for awhile."

"You just wait. The man of your dreams will show up when you're not looking for him."

11

"That phrase is complete bullshit. I'm just going to put that out there. Everybody says it to their single friends to give them hope. It's basically saying, 'Hey, try and not act so desperate and the men will come running.'"

"You are such a cynic sometimes." Leah rolled her eyes and set down the magazine.

"Easy for you to say, Miss Dating-a-Fabulously-Hot-Firefighter."

Leah grinned. "I still say you're a cynic."

Maybe she was, but she kind of had a right to be. She'd done nothing but strike out with the men she'd dated, having left some relationships with her confidence knocked down a notch.

Kenneth was no exception, probably because the sex between them had been awful. Which was likely the reason they'd stopped dating. Fortunately their friendship had survived...or had it? At first she'd thought so, but now she had to wonder if Kenneth pulling away was due to Ashley coming into the picture.

"Are you still thinking about Kenneth?"

Allison shrugged. "I don't get it. He isn't the marrying type, and definitely not to someone like Ashley."

"If it bothers you this much, go on and ask him then. I hear they're having a dinner at Burnham's tonight."

Allison made a not-so-silent harrumph. "Don't tempt me."

"Who me? Never." Leah waggled her eyebrows innocently.

Allison started to laugh, but turned her head into the sleeve of her blouse as another round of coughs racked her body.

"Gosh, that sounds awful, Allison. You should have canceled today. You need to be home in bed."

"Ugh. This is the tail end. It's nothing now. A few days ago I was knocked on my ass." She stared at her toes, now shiny with polish and drying.

Why couldn't she stop thinking about Ken marrying Ashley? It wasn't hard to see what Ashley saw in him—Ken was sexy, rich and a member of the prestigious Williams family. He was probably at the top of the list for every unattached girl in Seattle. But why on earth would *he* pick Ashley? The only thing she had was a sleazy reputation and probably a police record.

Maybe she *should* talk to Ken. It was time to figure out why he'd been blowing off their usual Monday lunch dates...

"What are you thinking?" Leah asked suspiciously. "I know that look in your eyes."

"Nothing." Allison gave an innocent smile. "So what time did you say this dinner is tonight? You know, just in case..."

Allison climbed out of her car and faced the front of Burnham's Seafood restaurant, her pulse quickening. Maybe she shouldn't be here...should've taken the hint when she'd tried to call Kenneth and his number had been changed.

Or maybe the fact you weren't even invited to his wedding.

But damn it this was *wrong*. They were friends. What was going on with Kenneth?

She lifted her chin and hurried up the steps, holding her head high as the doorman opened the door for her.

"Thank you," she murmured and stepped past him into the air-conditioned building, smoothing the skirt of her red dress down.

The interior of the upscale dining spot was dark with hardwood floors and mahogany tables spread about. She scanned the room until she found what she was looking for. The private room in the back.

Fortunately there were windows, and she could see the small party gathered inside. Fifteen, maybe twenty people. Most likely just friends and family of the Williams.

"Excuse me, ma'am, do you have a reservation?"

Allison jerked her gaze back to the waif-like-model in front of her. Hmm. Maybe it would be good to get a table first, then find the perfect moment to launch the meeting.

"Actually, I don't. My fiancé suggested meeting here for dinner tonight," she lied, tilting her head to give a hesitant smile. "You wouldn't happen to have a table available, would you?"

"Hmm." The hostess glanced down at the podium in front of her. "I think we can accommodate that. A table for two?"

"That would be wonderful. Thank you."

"Did you want to wait for your fiancé, or—?"

"If you don't mind, I think I'll wait at the table. He's notorious for being late."

"All right," the hostess nodded and stepped away from the podium. "Follow me."

The hostess led her to a small table where a floating candle lay flickering in the middle. Allison sat down and took the menu she was handed.

"Thank you."

"You're welcome. Your waiter will be with you shortly."

Once the hostess disappeared, Allison raised the menu in front of her just high enough to cover all of her face except her eyes.

Peering over the leather folder, she scanned the room only feet away from her now. They were all there. The Williams family and a few of Kenneth's close friends she recognized.

Shrill, high-pitched laughter drifted through the glass window just as a flash of bright red hair appeared from the corner of the room. All eyes were on the bride-to-be, who wore a floral sundress with a crown on her head.

Allison narrowed her gaze and made an inaudible harrumph. A crown? Really? And Kenneth's parents were beaming like he actually *was* marrying royalty. Maybe they were just happy he was settling down.

She shook her head. Had she stepped into the Twilight Zone? This was all just too weird.

"Hello there."

With a startled gasp, she turned her head and looked up at a male server who'd appeared next to the table.

"I'm Jordan, and I'll be your server today. Can I get you something to drink while you wait for the other half of your party?"

"Mmm. I think just water for now."

The server gave a brief nod, and she didn't miss the male appreciation in his gaze as he gave her a brief smile.

"Very good. I'll return shortly."

Generally she would have been flattered by his attention—she'd grown used to male interest over the years. Ever since the day she'd decided to drop the tomboy image and embrace all things girly. Makeup, dresses, manicures. Since she'd gone from being invisible, to being somewhat sexy by today's standards.

The server disappeared and she jerked her gaze back to the room, watching the people inside like they were some kind of exhibit in a zoo.

Kenneth, Kenneth, Kenneth. Where was the guy? She skimmed the room. Lord, look at all the pretty men. It looked like a freaking Ralph Lauren convention. Maybe he'd—*there.*

She narrowed her eyes as he appeared from behind a group of people and slipped his arms around Ashley, who giggled even louder.

"How did you do it, Ashley?" she muttered.

"Your water."

Allison resurrected her smile and took the glass of water from the server, wondering if he'd heard her comment.

"Would you like to order something to start with? Our calamari is a very popular choice. Or we have—"

"I'm fine." She winced at the edge in her voice. *Easy girl.* She glanced up at the server through her lashes and murmured in her best husky voice, "Thank you, Jordan. I'll signal you if I need anything else."

A flush stole up his neck and he gave a brisk nod before scurrying away.

Good. Hopefully he'd let her be for a bit. She turned her gaze back to the room, just in time to see the bride-to-be plant a wet kiss on Kenneth's mouth. And he *allowed* that? Kenneth hated PDAs.

Allison scowled, but her frown died as Kenneth stood to leave the room. *This* was her chance for an intervention.

Lowering her menu, she waited until he'd passed by her on the way to the bathroom, then stood to follow after him.

Before she'd taken two steps, strong fingers wrapped around her arm, halting her progress.

"Long time no see," Clint murmured.

Her eyes widened, but she didn't protest as her old friend tugged her through the restaurant.

In an empty hallway, out of view of the diners, he came to an abrupt halt and she bumped into him.

"Clint?" His name fell from her lips in dismay. She still couldn't quite believe he was here, but then why wouldn't he be? He'd been Kenneth's best friend when they were kids.

Just seeing Clint again robbed her of the ability to speak. It had to have been at least a year since they'd seen each other.

She ran her gaze over him. Black hair just a bit too long, piercing blue eyes, and a tall—at least several inches over six feet—muscled body. Apparently being a forest ranger agreed with him. He hadn't looked this good last time, had he? Or maybe he had and she just hadn't been looking?

The realization that he still held her arm blinked her back to reality and her thoughts dissipated into annoyance. Why had he dragged her across the restaurant like she'd been ready to shoot it up?

"What are you doing?" she asked.

He arched a brow and smiled, but the gesture didn't seem to hold much humor. "I was just going to ask you the same thing, Allie. Last I checked you weren't invited to this dinner."

Allison's cheeks burned with the reminder. So it was like that, was it? At one time she, Kenneth and Clint had been thick as thieves. She'd grown up just houses away from Kenneth, and Clint—who was originally from Montana—had always spent the summers with his grandma who lived next door to Kenneth's family. Even after college Clint had still come out. It was a habit he hadn't broken.

It was only when she and Kenneth had started dating that Clint had stopped making the trip to Washington state. Hadn't really replied to any of her emails either, just a short reply. Not unfriendly, but definitely not what they'd once had. It had saddened her, made her wonder if he just felt like the third wheel and didn't want to hang out?

But that was months ago now. Why was he acting like such a dick now?

She gave Clint a slight shrug and said, "What dinner? I have no idea what you're even talking about. Now if you'll excuse me, I was just on my way out."

"But you haven't yet eaten."

Now how did he know that? *Oh.* She drew in a slow breath. He'd been watching her. Watching her watch them. She should've known better. Clint had always been perceptive as all hell.

He laughed, and the sound came out low and a bit sexy, sending little shivers down her spine. "You can't expect me to believe that you showing up during Ken and Ashley's dinner is purely coincidence."

He cut right to the quick, didn't he? Deciding on a different technique, and wanting to erase any of his suspicions, she relaxed and let her mouth curl into a smile.

"Actually, yes."

"All right. Well, since you were on your way out, let me walk you."

Had he always been this bossy? Her smile disappeared and she glanced back in the private room. Maybe if she—

"Allison." This time her name was a silky warning on his lips.

As she watched, Kenneth left the bathroom and returned to the private room, never seeing her or Clint at the other end of the hallway.

Well, shit. Annoyance flickered through her and she scowled. *Thanks, Clint, for screwing up my plans.* Who knew when she'd get a chance to meet with Kenneth alone now?

Frustrated with Clint blocking her efforts and not wanting to make a scene, she gave a sharp nod and allowed Clint to lead her out the entrance of the restaurant.

Once in the parking lot she tugged her arm away.

"There, you walked me outside. I hope it was good for you." She rummaged in her purse for her keys. "As much as I'd like to catch up with you and chat, I should be on my way now."

Two hands came to rest on either side of her and she drew in a startled breath. Clint stepped forward, boxing her in between his body and her Toyota.

"Let me just make one thing clear, Allie." His words brushed hot across her face, and a tremble ran through her. God, was it his cologne or aftershave that smelled so good? Whatever it was, was rich and masculine, teasing her senses and slowing her thoughts.

Clint, this is Clint. Not some hot guy you're hitting on at a bar. How weird she was having this reaction to him. Maybe because it had been a year and she hadn't realized how much she missed him. Though right now she was kind of just wishing he'd go away again.

"Make what clear?" she finally asked, shaking her head so she could think straight again.

"It took Ken a long time to get over you, but he's clearly moved on." His gaze locked with hers, no amusement, just sober determination.

"What?" Her mouth gaped. "Are you serious? Kenneth never—"

"Look. Just take my advice. Stay away from him now. Whatever you're thinking, just stop it. He's getting married to someone else."

She quirked an eyebrow before folding her arms across her chest.

"What is *wrong* with you? I thought we were all friends. Why are you acting like I'm some crazy party crasher?"

"Times have changed, Allison. We've all changed. And if you were still such a good friend he would've invited you to the wedding and tonight's dinner."

Times have changed. Why did hearing him utter those words make her heart twist a little? When had everything gotten so complicated?

Unfortunately now wasn't the time to bring that up. Now was the time to try and save Kenneth's ass from a crappy future. Deciding to drop any pretense of not knowing about the dinner, she said, "And I'm sure he would've invited me tonight, if Ashley hadn't told him not to."

Skepticism flashed in Clint's eyes. "Why on earth would she do that?"

"Because she knows I don't like her."

"And why don't you like her?"

Maybe it would be better to tell him, possibly gain an ally. At this point what could it hurt trying to explain her rationale?

"Why? Because she's a trashy gold digger, Clint. I have a feeling she's faking a pregnancy to get him to marry her."

Clint stared at her for a moment, his expression unreadable. Hope sparked inside her and she held her breath.

"Really?" he finally said deadpan. "That's the best you got?"

Allison let out a growl of frustration and glared at him. "Oh, I shouldn't have said anything to you. I don't know why you don't trust me anymore."

"I just don't trust your motives."

"Don't you have a dinner to go to?"

"Yes. I do." He smiled, seeming amused by her loss of temper now.

"Then why don't you go."

"I will." He dipped his head, until those lips just about brushed her ear. "Just remember what I said, Allie."

Her pulse jerked and heat spread through her body. Shocked at her reaction, she raised her hand to push him back, but before she could touch him he'd pulled his arms away and released her.

"Good to see you again, Allison. We should do lunch and catch up," he called out, running his gaze over her one last time before he turned and crossed the parking lot to jog back into the restaurant.

Do lunch? That had to be the weirdest encounter ever with Clint. He'd been aggressive and cocky. Not like the easygoing Clint she'd used to spend time with. Did hanging out with bears in the woods all day jack up his freaking testosterone or something?

And the way he was dressed in jeans and a worn-out looking T-shirt, he must've stuck out like a flea on a poodle at the dinner tonight. Not that he looked bad—far from it—but as a friend of the Williams family you think he'd try a little harder. But then that's always how Clint had been. He always walked his own line.

She wrapped her fingers around the oversized heart keychain and jerked it from the bag. After unlocking her car, she climbed inside and drew in a deep breath.

Where did she go from here? She glanced back at the restaurant and drew her lip between her teeth.

Maybe she *should* just back off and leave Kenneth to his fate. But now that Clint had told her to back off, she was more inclined to keep going forward, if no other reason than just to piss *him* off. Clint's behavior was seriously annoying. Who the hell did he think he was?

There was a week until the wedding, she still had time. Allison shook her head and started her car, considering her options.

Chapter Two

Clint lingered inside the door of the restaurant, watching Allison as she climbed into her car. She didn't leave immediately, and he prepared himself to walk out and go another round with her.

Would she try and come back inside? He'd barely thought it, when a second later she started her car and backed out of the parking spot—tires squealing.

She was upset. He fought a smile and shook his head. Not that he could blame her. She'd seemed all too determined to walk up to Kenneth and try to...what, get him back?

His teeth snapped together. Even now, over a year later, the thought of Allison and Kenneth together gave him the urge to kick something. It just seemed...wrong. And it had been a little too hard seeing them together, so he'd stopped visiting.

He hadn't even realized they'd broken up until recently when Kenneth had announced he was engaged. And to a woman who was obviously not Allie. He'd told himself it wasn't relief he'd felt.

But if by some chance Allison *had* showed up tonight to fight for Kenneth, then she was seriously deluding herself.

He turned and headed back to the private room, though in truth the break from the nauseating dinner had been needed.

Any Williams gathering was about as fun as a proctology conference.

Allison might have left the restaurant, but her image lingered in his head. She'd looked fantastic tonight in that clingy red dress. She was a woman who knew exactly how to flaunt her curves—and she had them in spades.

He loved that about her. She'd never tried to shrink her body into society standards. Why did women always strive to be stick thin? Didn't they realize most men wanted a little meat to hold on to?

He'd thought she'd been off limits for the past year. When two of their group of three had split off into a couple, Clint had known things would never be the same. Partly because he was still jealous Kenneth had moved in on Allie when Clint was tempted to do the same. She'd been emotionally vulnerable, recovering from a bad break up, but he'd wanted her. Damn, how he'd wanted her. But Ken had moved in first, plucking her up like a wounded animal.

But they weren't together anymore. Hadn't been in quite a while. And Clint hadn't imagined the sexual tension between them tonight. She'd watched him in the way he used to dream she'd watch him. With awareness that he was a hot-blooded man. As if she'd wanted to know what it felt like to kiss him. He'd been tempted to lower his mouth to hers and find out if the chemistry between them ignited when their lips touched.

A heavy weight settled in his chest and he shook his head. But that wouldn't be a good idea. Touching Allison would be opening the door to a hall he really shouldn't be going down. She wasn't his type. Not anymore. There was a time when she hadn't been so high maintenance. When they'd both laugh about the uptight Williams' parties and superior attitude they all carried.

But Allison had changed. She'd become *one* of them, a city girl through and through, probably afraid to mess up her hair, and wearing her self-entitlement like a badge. And though he might want her physically, he couldn't see himself with a girl like that. Not for more than a night or two anyway...

Clint tugged the door to the restaurant's private room open, and a wall of sound greeted him. Time to once again pretend he fit in with these rich, materialistic people whose main concern seemed to be making sure birds didn't shit on their Lexus. Once, long ago, Ken had been pretty cool too. Until his hormones had kicked in and his priorities had become chasing tail and milking his parents for money.

"Clint. Where did you go?"

He turned to face his once good friend, who seemed half drunk already, and gave an easy shrug.

"I thought I saw an old friend," he lied. Had Kenneth seen Allison? Likely not.

"Ah, good deal." Kenneth leaned toward him and lowered his voice. "You ready to see some action at my bachelor party tomorrow night? We're going to hook you up with some fine women, buddy."

Clint's lips twisted. The only *fine woman* he wanted right now had just driven out of the parking lot like a bat out of hell.

"Yeah. About that. I don't think I'll be able to make it to the bachelor party."

"Not make it?" Kenneth's eyes widened. "Oh come on, Clint. You never chill with me anymore, and this is going to be awesome. Trust me, you won't want to miss it. Promise me you'll show."

There was probably no way around it, still he tried to be ambiguous. "We'll see."

"Kenneth, what are you doing over here?" Ashley came up behind them, slipping her arm through her fiancé's. "You're behaving yourself, aren't you, honey bunny?"

"Of course, babe. Just having a talk with Clint." Kenneth cleared his throat and lowered his head to drop a kiss on her downturned mouth.

Ashley pulled away, looking much more pleased. "Good. Just think, before long we'll be husband and wife."

Clint hid a smile at the flicker of panic he spotted in Kenneth's eyes. Maybe it was Ashley's high-pitched baby talk she used on him, but he just couldn't understand what Ken saw in the woman. Well. Besides a freakishly large pair of fake breasts.

"You want some more champagne, honey bunny?"

Clint winced. He couldn't be the only one who thought she sounded like a chipmunk trying to be sexy.

"That'd be great. Thanks, Ashley."

Once the woman bounced away, Clint glancing at Ken again.

"So you're in love, huh?"

"I guess. And with Mom's ultimatum about me settling down or getting cut off, Ashley seemed a good fit." Kenneth smiled and leaned close and winked. "Besides, she lets me fuck her in the ass."

Clint closed his eyes and tried not to let the unwanted image invade his head. Kenneth had always been way too loose-lipped about his sex life. Which made him think about...

Don't ask about Allison. Don't even do it— "You ever see Allie?"

"Allison?" Kenneth shook his head, his expression pensive. "Not as much lately, Ashley's not too keen on her. For awhile, before Ashley, I kept thinking about trying to get Allison back, 'cause she was pretty hot. Always been a pretty cool girl." Kenneth grimaced. "Though I gotta say she wasn't all that great in bed."

Anger and something else dark—something close to jealousy—sparked in Clint's gut, and his jaw flexed. *Of course they slept together, what did you expect?*

But saying Allison was bad in bed? He thought about her mischievous and passionate side he knew still had to exist. And how her eyes had flashed anger at him when he'd boxed her in at the car a short while ago. How for the briefest second he'd been shocked to see the flicker of awareness in her gaze.

Allison bad in bed? He didn't buy it. Not for a minute. In fact it made him question how attentive Ken was with the women in his bed.

He bit back a sigh, almost wondering if Allison had a right to be worried about the wedding. But unlike Allie, he could admit it wasn't his business who and when Ken married.

Although he wasn't completely certain her concerns were over Kenneth marrying Ashley, but that he was getting married at all. Did Allison still hold feelings for him?

Clint's gut twisted and he tightened his grip around his champagne glass. Hopefully she'd back off—he'd warned her to. But the Allie he knew wouldn't have let that stop her. And in a way, he almost hoped she'd try again. It'd give him another reason to see her again...

His mouth twitched and he sought out the tray of shrimp.

"Don't do it, Allison," Leah pleaded over the phone. "Oh God, *please* don't do it. This is way too extreme. Just let him marry the bimbo."

"Too late. I'm already on my way."

"Oh my God. Men are crazy at bachelor parties. You're going to be over your head—"

"I'm going to be fine. I'll just sneak in posing as a stripper—because, come on, *someone* will have ordered one. Once I'm there I'll pull Kenneth aside right away and have a little chat with him..."

"How did you even find out where they were holding the party?"

"I've got connections. I'm friends with the sister of one of the guy's attending."

"Let it go. Please, Allison."

"Hey, even if you were joking when you suggested the idea, I thought it was perfect. And you have to admit it'll be pretty clever if I can pull it off."

"I'm not sure I'd use the word clever..."

Allison parked her car on the curb next to the house in the upscale Mercer Island neighborhood. "It's too late, I'm here already."

"Allison—"

"I'll call you later. Love ya." She closed her phone and adjusted the rearview mirror to check out her appearance.

Her stomach flipped with excitement as she adjusted the black wig and swiped another layer of dark red lip-gloss on.

Nothing to worry about. She'd be in and out in twenty minutes tops. There would be no clothes even close to being removed. Plus, it would be kind of fun to see firsthand what went on at a bachelor party. Maybe Clint would be there...damn. Where had that thought come from?

"Stop it," she scolded herself. "Clint has nothing to do with why you're here tonight."

Still, her pulse surged as she climbed out of the car and walked toward the house.

Clint tilted the beer to his lips and stepped back to avoid another drunken groomsman stumbling across the room.

The music pounded so loud his head had begun to resonate in time with it. Hell, what he wouldn't give for a Tylenol right about now.

A stripper had showed up at the party an hour earlier. A skinny redhead with perky breasts. All the men in the room salivated over her. Everyone but Clint. His mind still lingered on the curvy blonde he'd sent packing from the dinner the other night. He'd been surprised—and almost disappointed—that Allison hadn't made another attempt to see Kenneth.

A high-pitched giggle had him glancing over at Ken and the stripper gyrating on his lap. She certainly seemed to be lax on the no touching rule. Likely because everyone here knew who Kenneth Williams was—and the bottomless checking account linked to his name.

He jerked his gaze away from the tawdry scene which both repulsed him and yet didn't help the chronic state of arousal he'd been in since seeing Allison again. *Damn it.* He took another swig of beer and fought the images of what he'd like to do to Allie flickering in his head.

The doorbell rang and he sighed, checking his watch. He'd promised to drop by tonight. Surely he could leave and not catch too much flack for it.

"Another stripper? *Hell yeah.*"

Another one? Okay, it was officially time to get the hell out of here. Shoving a hand through his hair, Clint sighed and got up to leave. The men had crowded around the door, blocking the exit as they surrounded the woman trying to move inside.

He grabbed his jacket, casting a bored glance at the woman almost buried among the men. He spotted the long naked legs and black bobbed hair.

She finally pushed through the group, stumbling into the middle of the room and casting an irritated glance back at the men.

"Give a girl a second to catch her breath, boys," she said and smoothed down her skirt. "I'm here for the groom."

Clint slowed in his progress to get out the door, intrigued by the new addition to the party. Even across the room something about her sent the hairs on the back of his neck up in warning.

She looked like she was trying way too hard in the skimpy little cop costume.

Her legs were damn long underneath the white pleather skirt barely covering her bottom. Her breasts barely stayed inside the matching top only zipped halfway up.

Clint's attention never left her as she moved around the party. She kept glancing around nervously and swatting off the advances of any man who attempted to approach.

There was something about her... He set his jacket back down and moved through the party toward the new stripper.

"Hey, Kenneth boy, here's another one here for you," someone called out.

Kenneth glanced away from the redhead who was now kissing his neck, and turned his focus onto the new stripper.

His gaze moved over her almost in dismissal before he looked away.

"Little too Plain Jane for me. You boys have fun with her. I'm good with Trixie here."

Clint's jaw hardened and he sucked in a swift breath. Christ, Ken could be an asshole when he drank. Before looking back at the new woman, he already knew what he'd find. He turned to see anyway. The hurt on her face wasn't a surprise, but the blazing rage underneath certainly was. An expression he recognized all too well.

Holy hell. Shock ripped through him and he went rigid. He mentally removed the wig and dark makeup from the woman. The shock faded into a slow pulse of pleasure.

Allison had actually had the balls to try and crash Kenneth's *bachelor party.*

"How about dancing for me instead, baby?" One bold attendee approached her and reached out to touch her hip. "I'm a good tipper."

Allison spun around, a tight smile on her face as she pushed the man away.

"All in good time, buddy. I need to go freshen up first." Her gaze skittered around the room and landed on Clint.

Clint slid his attention away from her, raising the beer to his mouth as he tried to appear only mildly interested. As if he hadn't recognized her. Part of him was tempted to march right over to Allison and yank that wig off her head and push her out the door again. Who did she think she was fooling?

Actually, that was damn obvious. Everyone. Likely the only people in this room who would recognize her were him and Kenneth. And Ken was way too inebriated to look that closely at the stripper. Not to mention he'd just written her off as a Plain Jane.

What was Allie's intention tonight in showing up at the party? Was she going to be that blatant in an effort to seduce Kenneth? He turned his head again to look and see what she was doing now and his pulse quickened.

She'd disappeared. He slid his gaze around in search of white pleather and long legs. Hell, where had she gone?

He set his beer down and moved through the crowded room. After glancing down an empty hallway he was about to search the game room when he heard a noise come from one of the bedrooms.

Clint took a hesitant step down the hallway toward the sound.

"Just back off—" Allison's sharp words ended in a muffled shriek.

Damn. He sprinted toward the open door to the room. When he stepped inside his gut clenched and his pulse jumped.

With a growl, he rushed across the room and grabbed the shirt of the man who had Allison pinned against the wall. With one tug, he'd lifted the man and flung him a few feet away.

"Hey, man—"

"Get the hell out of here," he snarled, recognizing the groomsman who'd been trying to feel up Allison when she'd first walked in.

"Damn. What's your problem?" The man slurred his words and stumbled toward the door, casting an irritated glance at Allison. "She's just a fucking stripper."

Clint took one step toward the man, fists clenched, before the guy scrambled out of the room with a yelp.

He drew in a slow breath in an attempt to lower his blood pressure, before turning to confront Allison. Had the other guy touched her? Hurt her? Concern had his brows drawing together. And anger at her that she'd been stupid enough to try and sneak in as a stripper with a bunch of drunken men.

"Excuse me."

He caught her hand right as she tried to scurry past him, her head lowered.

"Hold up there," he said gruffly. "Are you okay? Did he hurt you?"

She kept her head down, but gave a slight shake of her head. "I'm fine."

Clint frowned. Did she realize he knew who she was? She certainly was doing everything to avoid looking at him.

She tugged at her hand and cleared her throat. "Can I have my hand back, please?"

"In a moment." He decided to play along with her act for a moment. "What company do you work for?"

Her shoulders tensed. After a moment she muttered, "At the same place the other girl works."

"I didn't realize they'd ordered two strippers."

"You're right. It was obviously a misunderstanding. I'll just head out." She stepped away, tugging at her hand again, but he didn't release it.

"Not so fast. You did drive all the way out here." He moved his thumb over the rapidly beating pulse on her wrist. "How about a private dance?"

Her head did jerk up this time, her eyes flashing.

It was damn hard to bite back a smile, but Clint managed it. He also made sure there would be no recognition in his gaze. He looked her over, appreciation the only emotion she'd be able to read in his eyes.

The suggestion had been more of a joke, but his voice had sounded too husky. Made the question more intimate and legitimate.

Damn, she was sexy. Sexy and vulnerable. Obviously she'd realized she was in over her head at this party. Beneath the thick makeup her hazel eyes were wide with anger and alarm. The exposed curves of her breasts rose and fell with her uneven breathing.

His dick tightened beneath his jeans as he inhaled the floral fragrance of her perfume. She'd even shown up wearing the same scent she always wore. She sure wasn't trying very hard to stay incognito.

The next breath he dragged in wasn't quite as steady either. Jesus, he wanted her. In every way. He should just pull off her wig and tell her to get the hell out of here. Didn't she realize the trouble she could've gotten into? Would've gotten into if he hadn't walked in?

He should tell her, but he wouldn't. Not yet, anyway.

His thumb moved over her pulse again and he made a murmur of triumph at her soft moan. The flare of arousal in her eyes made him stop fighting it. He wanted Allie, and after all these years, it was time he had her.

"So what do you say to that dance, kitten?"

Allison's head spun and her knees turned into rubber. Each time Clint's thumb moved across her wrist another wave of sweet tingles would race through her body.

He wanted her to give him a private dance. Wait, not her. A stripper. He hadn't even recognized her. Should she be offended? They'd known each other since they were kids. Or maybe she should just be relieved her costume was convincing?

Part of her, a small completely crazy and random part, wanted to push him down onto the edge of the bed and dance until he was begging. The sense of empowerment made her heady, and it would be fantastic and kind of funny to see Clint beg. Her body zinged with fire. Her breasts felt heavier. The idea of tempting Clint and herself with this insane chemistry between them was all too real. All too crazy, but real. And she wanted to dance for him like he'd just invited.

Of course, that would be just plain stupid. Not to mention she couldn't dance for shit.

"Dance for me," he commanded again and slid his hand to her waist, pulling their bodies snug together.

She swallowed hard and tried to form a coherent thought. Or at least some kind of response a stripper would say.

"I...I don't do private dances."

He nuzzled her ear, his fingers moving up and down the space between her hip and ribcage. "You could make an exception for me."

No. No. No. She lifted her hands to his chest, determined to push him away, but then his lips brushed the curve of her ear and her fingers grazed his hard torso. She caught her breath and suddenly she was clenching the fabric of his shirt.

His lips closed over the curve of her ear, just before his tongue moved out to stroke her lobe. Fire singed her blood and her mind turned to mush. Allison let her head roll back, giving him access to her throat.

This is Clint. Clint *for God's sake.*

He gave a soft growl of approval, and his mouth moved to the curve of her neck closing over the flesh and sucking softly.

The burning heat spread through her body, sending a heavy ache between her legs at the continued assault of his tongue and lips. He traced a finger into her cleavage and her panties went damp with her desire.

"Clint." His name left her lips on a frantic plea.

She froze. She'd said his name. Oh God. Maybe he hadn't noticed...

"Yes, Allie?"

Ice rushed down her spine, conflicting with the heat that burned her cheeks.

"Let go of me." She pushed against his chest and stumbled backward, almost tripping in her heels. "You knew it was me? For how long?"

He arched one eyebrow, the disbelief in his gaze answer enough. He looked completely unruffled by their heated moment. As if it hadn't affected him nearly as much as it had her.

She exhaled slowly through her nostrils. God, she really hated him right now. He'd just been toying with her. Like a cat with a bug. Only it was kind of messed up that the bug had liked it.

Who would've known Clint's lips on her would've made her feel like *that*?

"You knew it was me and you still...touched me like that?"

His steady gaze darkened in a way that had her breath catching, instead of answering he said, "You're leaving this party. Now, Allison. This is a bachelor party, and unless you intend to start strip—"

She gasped. "I am *not* stripping, you jerk!"

"I didn't think so. Let's go." He caught her wrist, tugging her toward the door.

She dug in her heels and refused to budge. "No. I need to talk to Kenneth."

"Call him tomorrow."

She blinked, hating to admit the truth. "He changed his number."

"And didn't give it to you?" he mocked. "Why not drop by his house?"

"Because he's moved into a place with Ashley and I don't know where. What, you think I didn't try the obvious stuff already? She's *keeping* me from him."

Clint's lips twitched. "Okay, Allison, I'm gonna say it. You're acting kind of stalkerish."

"I am not stalkerish," she growled and tried to pull free. "I'm concerned about our friend—which at least *one* of us should be. Let me go, I'll talk to Kenneth myself."

"No can do." He pulled her toward the door.

"Clint, *stop*. You can't keep dragging me out of places."

"Okay. I won't drag you." He released her arm, only to grab her around the waist and scoop her up. "I'll carry you out."

"What the—ooph!" She gasped as he dropped her over his shoulder, and marched her back into the living room.

"Hey, look at that!" Someone yelled. "Clint's taking the stripper home!"

"No fair, buddy. You need to share."

"Now that is one fine ass. Can't I have a piece, Clint?"

Allison's mouth hung open, humiliation zinging through her as she realized her skirt was up over her waist now, showing off her white bikini panties.

She was going to kill Clint. Once he got her outside, of course. Because she had to give him credit for realizing that sticking around with these drunken ass clowns probably wasn't a good idea at this point.

The front door opened, assailing her with a cool late night breeze, before it slammed shut behind them as they moved outside. He didn't set her down, just continued to carry her down the driveway until they'd reached her car.

Only then did he slide her back up over his shoulder. But instead of just setting her down, he slid her with agonizing slowness down the length of his body. Her breasts scraped against his hard chest, her pelvis hit flush against his and there was no mistaking the hard length of his erection beneath his jeans.

Despite the cool summer night, her body flooded with warmth and when her feet finally touched the pavement, she stumbled away from him just as turned on as she'd been back in the room.

"Do you have your keys?" he asked flatly.

"Maybe you should have asked me that before we left the party."

"Do you?"

"Yes." She glared at him, but fished into the bodice of her costume to retrieve the key to her car. She'd left everything else tucked under her front seat.

His gaze followed the movement and she bit off a frustrated curse. Her nipples peaked under his close scrutiny, rubbing against the plastic of the costume. Wearing a bra had been impossible with the top, but fortunately it had been tight enough to support her full breasts.

He lifted his gaze from her chest and under the streetlight she didn't miss the desire in his gaze. Then he stepped closer to her. Her heart skipped and she took a quick step backwards, her bottom hitting the passenger door.

Clint reached up, his palm gently cupping the side of her face.

"Come back to my hotel room."

The air locked in her lungs and Allison's heart nearly stopped. Hot awareness rocked through her as his offer resonated in her head. Had she heard that wrong?

"We would be explosive together, Allie," he murmured, tracing his thumb over her lower lip. "Tell me you haven't thought about it."

She tried to shake her head, but it just kind of twitched as a low moan formed in her throat. Clint wanted to sleep with her, wasn't even being all cautious, subtle or romantic about it. He was just laying it all on the table.

"I want you," he continued, "and I intend to have you, kitten."

Kitten. It was almost a sexual play on how he'd called her Allie-cat all those years. She'd seen Clint be aggressive with women before, but never with her. To have his attention focused on her was both titillating and a bit scary.

Her knees went weak and she closed her eyes, already seeing it in her mind. How going to bed with Clint would be. *But he's your friend.* And yet she'd crossed that boundary with Kenneth at one point, why not Clint?

Clint's mouth, soft and yet firm, pressed against hers. The moan in her throat finally escaped as his tongue slid deep inside to tease her.

Allison's thoughts scattered as pleasure slid through her body. Heating her, making every nerve come to life. She instinctively pressed herself close to him, wrapping her arms around his neck and responding to his kiss as if it were the most natural thing to do.

The hard press of Clint's erection against her belly sent an ache pulsing low between her legs.

He lifted his head and dazedly she saw the hard glitter of arousal in his eyes.

"Let's go to my hotel room, Allie. You can drive me back here to my car in the morning."

It took a second for his words to sink in, but when they did a flush stole into her cheeks. Did he seriously just expect her to waltz out of here and go to bed with him?

A thought slid through her, leaving her chilled and her stomach twisting. Or was Clint just looking at sex as distraction? As a way to keep her from talking to Kenneth while getting a little action himself? Would Clint really be that calculating?

Swallowing the unease, Allison shook her head. Either way, she wasn't going to jump into bed with Clint. It could only lead to trouble.

"Sorry, Clint. That's just not a good idea."

His lips curved into a sexy smile, before he dipped his head to nip at her bottom lip again. "You want *me* to drive?"

She pressed her hands against his chest to push him away. "No, I want you walk back into that party and tell Kenneth to come out here for a minute."

Clint stilled and all traces of arousal disappeared from his eyes. A small tic started in his jaw. "Leave him alone, Allison."

"I can't. Not until I've spoken with him."

He exhaled harshly. "I don't think this has anything to do with him marrying Ashley, but everything to do with him *not* marrying you."

What? Her mouth flapped and she shook her head. Didn't Clint know she'd only dated Ken for a few months and it had been a terrible idea? Any relationship between them was water under the bridge.

"You're way off base," she muttered. Her chin lifted and she felt a totally irrational desire to push his buttons. She knew she was being ridiculous, but didn't care. "And I'll talk to him if I have to show up at this house tomorrow and drag his hungover ass off the couch."

His eyes flared with a cross between amusement and aggravation. He plucked the keys from her hand and unlocked her door. "No, you won't. And this is your last warning, Allison." He lifted a finger in front of her face. "Contact him again and I'm done playing nice."

She climbed into the car and glared up at him. "This was *nice*, Clint? Once upon time you used to be nice. But this was-"

He shut the door with a wink, cutting off her tirade.

What a *jerk*. Allison's teeth snapped together as she started the engine, before pulling away from the curb.

She'd show Clint *exactly* what he could do with his warning.

Chapter Three

Not even twelve hours later, Allison sat in her car outside the bachelor party house again. The house belonged to one of the groomsmen, but Kenneth's car was still parked out front.

She would talk to Kenneth this morning, if it was the last thing she did.

Is this really about Kenneth anymore, or goading Clint? a little voice in her head wondered, but she snuffed it out. Of course it was about Kenneth. She cared about his future, even if he'd been all too quick to shut her out of his life.

He called you a Plain Jane.

Ugh. She'd make him regret that little comment, though God knows he'd feel terrible if he realized who he'd really been insulting.

Allison slipped out of her car and drew in a steadying breath. Her heels clicking on the driveway were the only sound on the quiet Saturday morning as she crossed.

She'd almost reached the front door when the hum of an engine had her turning around. An SUV came to an abrupt stop outside the house.

Her pulse jumped to life and a smile curved her mouth. She wiped it away, surprised and yet not really that Clint had shown up to stop her. Had he been staking out the house or something?

He sat in the driver's seat, the sunglasses he wore shielding his gaze. Was he hungover?

He rolled down the window and yelled. "Get in."

"What?"

"Get in," he repeated. "If you want to see Kenneth, then I'll take you to where he is."

"Where he is? But his car's here." She narrowed her gaze and walked back down the driveway toward him. "And why are you suddenly willing to help me?"

Clint sighed and looked away. "Because I've been doing some digging, and you may be right about this Ashley woman. I'm having some doubts of my own. Ken's having breakfast with some guys over at the Hilton, we can drive over there and talk to him."

She watched him for a moment, not completely sure she trusted him, but if Clint really had done some research he would've discovered what kind of sleaze Ashley was.

"The Hilton?" She arched a brow and glanced down the road. The Hilton was only a few miles away. And she could always jump out at a stop sign if he tried any funny stuff.

Clint reached across and opened the passenger door, so it swung open toward her. "Come on."

Allison gave a terse nod and climbed inside the SUV. Settling on the leather seat she glanced over at him and fastened her seatbelt.

"I still don't really trust you," she muttered and fluffed her hair.

Clint hit the gas, pulling a U-turn and heading in the direction of the hotel.

"I think we should just sit him down and explain our worries," she said. "It depends how far she's pulled the wool over his eyes. Or however that phrase goes, ya know?"

She glanced over at him to see him nod.

"How long did you stay at the party last night?"

"Left shortly after you did."

"Oh." She frowned. "So you just came back to meet the guys for breakfast?"

He didn't answer and the first prick of unease hit her.

"They're not really at breakfast are they?"

"I don't really know, Allie," he finally admitted lightly. "They very well could be."

"You son of a bitch," she growled.

Okay, that was it. Time to jump out at the next light. He slowed the car a moment later and she went to pull the door handle, just as she heard it lock shut.

Her pulse began to thud faster as the light turned green and the SUV sped up again.

"You said you'd take me to see him."

"I'll take you, Allie." His lips twitched. "And you'll like it."

She almost snorted at the bad sexual innuendo, but was starting to realize there wasn't much humor in her situation.

"You didn't dig into Ashley's background. And you were never going to take me to him, were you?"

He shook his head, his smile dimming. "No, Allison, I wasn't. And I can't believe you thought for one minute I would."

Gee, did he really have to reiterate how stupid she'd just been?

"You know I have to say, I'm a little surprised you were that easy," Clint said, glancing over at her with a wide smile.

She gripped the handle on the door as the SUV took a sharp corner. "Don't call me easy."

His deep laughter sent little shivers through her and her mouth went dry.

"And you were right to say you didn't trust me, kitten." He shrugged. "You shouldn't. I gave you your last warning last night."

That unease in her gut turned into a heavy ball.

"Let me out of the car."

"I can't do that."

"Why not?" The anger in her belly burned hotter and she tried to pull up the lock but he locked it again.

"You're not honestly considering jumping out of a moving vehicle, are you, Allie?"

Allison gave a growl of frustration and slapped her palm against the window.

"This is ridiculous." She stared out at the blur of trees as they sped down a deserted road. "Where are we going?"

"Away," he answered ambiguously.

"Away," she mimicked him. "We're going away? What the *hell* kind of answer is that?"

"The only answer you're getting right now. And watch your mouth. I know your mom taught you better."

"Didn't your mom teach *you* that kidnapping is a *felony*?" she shot back and slapped the window again.

"If you break my window it's going to seriously piss me off, Allie."

"Well, guess what? I'm already pissed." *Slap.* Her hand connected with the glass again and again. "Maybe you should have taken that into account when you abducted me, Clint."

45

She nearly fell out of her seat as he swerved the car to the side of the road.

Was he going to let her go? Leave her stuck on some random back road? Hell, she didn't care, she'd hike her way back to her car if she had to.

He climbed out of the vehicle and came around her side, wrenching open the door.

"Get out."

Relief flooded through her. He *was* letting her go. Finally. She scooted out the door, making the jump down to the ground and smoothing her dress back down her thighs.

"Well, it's about time you came to your senses—oh!"

He jerked her hard against him, both of her wrists in one of his massive hands.

"Maybe I didn't make myself clear," he murmured, his gaze full of determination and something else...something hot. Something that sent a jolt of heat straight from her stomach to between her legs.

Her pulse quickened and she dragged in a shuddering breath, tugging at her hands.

"Have you gone completely insane?" she whispered.

"Maybe." His lips twisted. "Or maybe I'm just willing to go to any lengths to make sure you don't break up Kenneth's wedding."

"I'm not..." She ran her tongue over her suddenly dry lips. "Wait, Kenneth's wedding isn't until next week."

"Exactly. And that means we'll have one whole week to catch up, kitten."

Clint watched her eyes widen with shock and he almost felt sorry for her—almost. Except he'd warned her multiple times and she needed to be stopped.

Taking her out of the equation had been an idea he'd been playing with since she'd threatened to show up at the house this morning. And the more he thought about it, the better the idea had seemed.

He'd been ready, sitting in his SUV parked down the street and drinking coffee, waiting to see if she really had the balls to show up again. Not really thinking she would, but somewhat excited when she did.

"Clint, you can't do this," she choked, her body beginning to tremble. "This is kidnapping."

"Yeah, you said that already."

"You can't take me away for *a week*." She tugged at her wrists again, and he tightened his hold. "Oh my God. You've gone loony, Clint. You're—argh."

Her knee connected with his shin and he winced, pushing her back against his SUV.

"Stop it," he said, irritated now. He tried not to think about how soft her body was against him and how her breasts pressed against his chest. "I'm not the one trying to break up a wedding."

Her eyes flashed with frustration and fury. "You can't play God, Clint."

"And neither will you, Allie. Even if I have to see to it."

She lowered her gaze and he watched her small pink tongue sweep across her lush mouth again. He bit back a groan. Man, she looked sexy when she did that. And she did it a lot.

"Okay," her tone calmed significantly. "You're right. Of course you're right. Why don't you take me back to my car and I'll just drive home. Deal?"

His chest shook with laughter and he shook his head. How stupid did she think he was? Did she honestly think she could pull out that docile act to convince him she'd changed her mind? He knew her way too well for that.

"No deal. I can't take that risk. I don't trust you any further than I can spit, kitten."

"Stop calling me kitten," she yelled and tried to—*oh hell no she didn't*—knee him in the groin.

He pressed his body harder against her, making sure she couldn't move. She glared at him, her mouth drawn tight and her breasts rising and falling with each breath she jerked in.

"Besides," he continued softly, and gave her a slow smile. "A week together means we can take up where we left off last night."

"If you think I would *ever* go to bed with you after—"

"I don't think, I know, Allie. And I'm pretty sure you know it too."

He reached out and ran a finger down the side of her soft cheek, and she sucked in a swift breath. He watched the heat flicker in her eyes and knew she could—and probably would—deny it until she was blue in the face, but Allison wanted him.

"I repeat. You're loony."

He laughed again. "I will bring you back here, but not until Ashley and Ken have exchanged their vows."

"That's not until next week," she said again in a rush. "I have to be at work."

"No, you don't, teachers have summers off." He watched her eyes round with shock.

What, did she think he'd forgotten about the teaching job at a private school Kenneth had gotten her a couple of years ago? Whether she was the most qualified candidate or not, just the recommendation from a Williams family member—and money donated—was enough to guarantee her the position.

His thumb slid inward to stroke over her bottom lip. Her body trembled in the response. God, he wanted her.

"You have no right to do this to me, Clint. None. You're being a total jerk. This is just—"

He pulled his thumb away and replaced it with his mouth. Crushing his lips down on hers in a kiss to stop her tirade, and because he couldn't resist her any longer.

Her angry gasp parted her lips enough to let him slide his tongue into the moist cavern of her mouth. He tasted her. Warm, succulent and the spicy taste of cinnamon gum.

She struggled against him, each twist of her body brushed her breasts into contact with his chest. He slowed the kiss, rubbing his tongue against hers. The friction had his dick pulsing against his jeans and he ground himself against her stomach.

The fight in her seemed to disappear and she went slack in his arms. Her small moan sent a jolt of triumph through him and he released her wrists so he could grab her ass.

The swell of her bottom spilled over into his palms, and he squeezed the soft flesh, pulling her harder against him.

Allison. God he wanted her. Had wanted her for so many years now. He was tempted to take her here on the side of the damn road.

Crack. The sound reached him before the sting of her palm glancing across his cheek.

She wrenched her mouth away from his, and glared up at him, her gaze both hot and skittish.

His fingers dug into her ass cheeks and his jaw clenched. *Okay, maybe you deserved that.* Taking a deep breath, he counted to ten.

"You know what, Allie?"

"You're going to come to your senses and let me go?" she suggested with tight sarcasm.

"Oh, hell no, I'm gonna keep you." He slid one hand up her back and pushed her close, until her tight nipples rubbed against his chest. "And I think we're going to have a lot of fun together this week."

Panic flashed in her eyes again. "Where are you taking me? To some cheap hotel?"

"Absolutely not."

She watched him warily. "Then where? Because you know I'm going to run the first chance I get."

The sound of a car coming down the road finally encouraged him to step back from her. He opened the front door and urged her back inside.

She shook her head and climbed into the backseat instead, obviously not wanting to be anywhere near him at this point. His lips twitched into amusement.

"I've taken that into consideration. That you'll try and run and all." He climbed into the driver's seat. "And I have a feeling once we get there, you won't want to run off. Not alone anyway."

"Unless you're taking me to the fucking Venetian hotel in Vegas, I'm seriously going to have to disagree," she snapped, buckling up.

He gave a soft laugh and shook his head. Physically she was the epitome of a woman—wore dresses, makeup and had the lush curves of a pin up queen. And yet she had a mouth that would make a sailor cringe.

Clint started the SUV again. Yeah. He was going to enjoy spending time with Allie again. Quite a bit.

Where the hell were they going? Allison stifled a yawn and lifted her head from the window. How long had they been driving? The only thing she knew was they were going east. She'd driven over to Pullman to visit friends enough during her college days to realize that.

She glanced at her watch. Damn. They'd already been on the road for three hours.

"I'm hungry." Her words cut through the faint country music he had playing. "I don't suppose you planned my kidnapping enough to bring food?"

"There should be a granola bar in the backpack on the floor. And we'll be stopping for food in about another hour."

She leaned over and grabbed the backpack, rummaging through the bag for the granola bar. After she found it, she unwrapped it and took a bite. Ugh. When was the last time she'd eaten this stuff?

Chewing absently on the bar, she tried to block out the bland taste. Unfortunately it wasn't even one of those sugary, chocolate dipped kinds—because chocolate would have been good right about now. It was one that actually had health benefits, full of nuts and berries and shit.

She glanced at the back of Clint's dark head as he drove the SUV steadily down the two-lane road, singing a country song out of key.

When he'd kissed her, thrusting his tongue into her mouth and grinding his erection into her belly, she'd wanted to push her fingers into his thick dark hair. Pull him closer in a move that could help ease the ache between her legs.

Don't go there. You will not go there. Wanting to fuck the man who kidnapped you cannot be a good thing. I don't care how good of friends you used to be.

She ate the last bite of the granola bar and crumpled the wrapper in her hand. Then, even knowing it was petty and rebellious, she threw it at the back of his head.

Clint laughed as it bounced right back off and landed on the seat somewhere. She sighed and looked out the window.

What a mess. Kidnapped. And all because Clint was convinced she wanted Kenneth back and was crazy enough to break up his wedding. Maybe she did want to break it up, but it sure as hell wasn't because she wanted Kenneth back.

"Seriously." She sighed and leaned her head back against the seat. "I give up, Clint. I won't say anything to Kenneth. He can marry Ashley and get taken to the cleaners. I'll stay away from him all week—I promise."

"No can do, Allie." Clint turned up the volume on the radio.

"Well you suck." Frustration made the granola bar churn in her stomach and she ground her teeth together. If he wasn't taking her to a cheap motel, then where *was* he taking her?

"And I'm still running the first chance I get," she muttered under her breath.

No matter what it cost, she'd call a taxi, take a train or fly if needed. But there was no way she was—damn. He had her purse. It was sitting up front by him. She'd have to grab it back.

"How long were you planning this? To kidnap me?"

"As of last night when I gave you your final warning. And let's get rid of the word kidnap, okay? I prefer to think of it as two old friends just spending some time together."

Allison gave a snort of laughter and shook her head. "I'm calling a spade a spade." She clenched her hands into fists in her lap, trying not to think about what he had planned for the week. Or his statement that they'd be sleeping together. The image of it had her body trembling. "And I won't have sex with you. If that was your goal by this whole kidnapping thing."

"My goal, as I clarified earlier, was to keep you from breaking up the wedding." He gave a husky laugh. "Sleeping with you will be the bonus."

"*Clint.* I'm not sleeping with you."

"Whatever you say, kitten." He didn't sound the least bit unsure of himself.

She scowled. And why should he be? She'd lost herself in that kiss. She'd been ready to hike her dress around her hips, pull off her panties and jump him. That's what he'd done to her.

"You know, we got a later start than I thought we would." He sighed. "I think we may have to check into a cheap motel tonight after all."

"A motel?" Alarm slid through her. Visions of sharing one small room with him, having him shower just feet away. Oh God. This week...how was she going to make it through?

"Yeah." He pulled off the highway and turned into the parking lot of a small motel.

Gravel crunched under the tires of the SUV as he pulled up in front of the office.

"I'm going to go inside and get us a room." He turned around and winked. "Are you going to behave yourself?"

"Where the hell am I going to go?" She folded her arms across her chest. "We're in the middle of nowhere—which I'm sure is exactly how you planned it."

He stared at her for a moment, as if weighing how much he could trust her. *If you're smart, you won't trust me an inch, Clint.*

"I'll be back in five minutes." He climbed out of the vehicle and walked into the motel office.

But once he was inside the office for a few minutes she had second thoughts. Could she get away with it?

Just go.

Knowing too much time had already passed, she jerked open the car door and with one quick jump down to the ground, she was off running across the gravel parking lot.

Her heart pounded and her throat tightened. The ding of the bell from the office signaled he'd seen her escape attempt.

Shit!

Why? Why the hell did she have to be wearing heels right now?

"Allison."

He screamed her name from just inches behind her. She let out a groan of frustration and increased her strides, trying to reach the highway which was just feet away. The highway meant cars. Cars meant the possibility of—

Snap. Her heel broke off and she went flying toward the highway and directly into the path of an oncoming car.

Strong arms shot around her waist, jerking her back just as the vehicle whizzed by, horn blaring.

Her heart in her throat she went weak against him. Oh God. She'd been so close to getting hit.

"Jesus Christ, Allie." He spun her around and the fear in his own gaze was obvious. "Are you okay?"

"I'm okay." Her voice shook and she made no attempt to escape his arms this time.

Adrenaline and shock still raced through her blood, making her legs useless to support her own weight. She leaned into him, breathing in his spicy aftershave as she willed her heart rate to return to normal.

"Come on, let's go to the room. Do you want me to carry you?" His tone was almost regretful, even as his arms tightened around her.

Heat rushed into her cheeks and she jerked away. "I can walk, thank you very much."

She went to stride past him, and he caught her elbow.

"Walking is fine as long as I'm holding on to you."

He kept his hand wrapped around her arm and led her toward a room on the far side of the motel. Inwardly she cursed her own stupidity. For thinking it had been a good idea to run into oncoming traffic, rather than run into the motel office and simply explain she wasn't here willingly.

Although she was pissed at Clint, she didn't really want to have to call the police and tell them he'd kidnapped her. That could pretty much ruin his life. Which left her in a bit of a dilemma on how to get away from him.

"What did you tell the motel people? Surely they thought it was a bit odd you had to chase the woman traveling with you onto the highway."

"No, they didn't find it odd at all." His mouth twisted into a slight smile. "I told them I had just picked you up from the psych ward back in Seattle, and you still had some issues."

Her vision blurred red and she changed her mind about having him arrested.

"You are such an asshole."

"I actually think you're the first to tell me that." He reached the door to their room and slipped the key in. A second later he swung open the door.

The smell of stale smoke and dust tickled her nostrils as he forced her inside the room in front of him.

Clint flicked up the light switch, and her gaze traveled around the room. The blood left her head and she gripped the dresser.

"Where's the other bed?" She spun around to face him.

"They only had a king-sized room left." He dropped his keys on the dresser and turned the lock on the door, sealing her in with him.

"*No.*" She lunged at him with her fists clenched.

He caught her wrist, his eyes narrowing. "You already hit me once and I let you get away with it. I may not be as nice next time."

"I know you too well, Clint, you wouldn't hit a woman," she scoffed.

"No," he said quietly as his thumb moved over the pulse on the inside of her wrist. "I'd find a much more pleasant form of punishment."

Allison ignored the flutters in her belly. She lifted her chin and said, "I think I'd rather have you hit me."

"Liar." He laughed quietly and to her horror pulled her against him. "You liked it when I kissed you this morning."

"Not even a bit." Her pulse went into double time.

"And last night at the bachelor party? You were practically melting in my arms."

"Talking to girls like this doesn't actually get you laid, does it?"

"In fact," he went on like she hadn't even spoken, "I think you'd like it if I did a whole lot more than kiss you tonight."

The scent of him filled her senses, sending her mind spinning and making her knees tremble. His hard torso pressed firmly against her breasts and her nipples tightened into hard points against the lace of her bra. She swallowed hard and tugged at her wrist.

"Tell me, Allie. I've always wondered how you like it. Are you all about the romance?" His voice lowered to a soft caress. "Do you enjoy it when a man gently sucks on your nipples and brings you to orgasm while playing your clit like an instrument?"

His words sent a rush of hot moisture between her legs and she bit back a groan.

"Stop this," she begged hoarsely. "Please, Clint."

"Or do you like it hard?" he went on, ignoring her plea. "Do you want a guy to bite and suck on your nipples until they're red and marked?" He lowered his head, his breath hot against her cheek. "Do you like to hold a man's head between your legs—let him eat you as if you're the fucking blue ribbon pie at the fair?"

Shock ripped through her, from the top of her head to her toes which were curling. Shock and absolute lust. No man had ever spoken to her in such a crude, sexual way before. And more so, no man had ever fucked her hard like that. The idea of Clint being the one to do it and the imagery his words created...

This time a groan did escape and she could feel the dampness of her panties between her legs.

"Or maybe both." His eyes darkened and he used his free hand to pull her tighter against him. Through the abrasive fabric of his jeans she felt him growing harder against her belly.

"One thing is certain—I'm going to enjoy finding out." He slid his hand down her spine to her bottom, bunching the fabric of her dress.

Cool air tickled her buttocks, and her pulse quickened as he pulled the dress over her hips. His fingers plucked at the strip of thong between the cheeks of her ass.

"I was wondering about this." His mouth hovered just above hers. "Whether you wear thongs or just no panties at all."

"Both," her voice trembled, and she couldn't believe she was admitting it. "Sometimes a thong, sometimes nothing."

Why wasn't she pushing him away? She should be fighting this—fighting him. But at this moment nothing else mattered except being locked in this sensual power struggle with Clint.

She drew in a ragged breath and before she could reconsider, pressed her body firmly against his.

He gave a murmur of approval. "I've been wondering about another thing."

"Oh yeah?"

His lips brushed across hers, ever so lightly and a tremble racked her body.

"What's that?" She brushed her lips over his this time.

He followed the strip of her thong down with his fingers, low between her cheeks. With a slight tug, she felt him slip his finger beneath the fabric, before his fingers grazed over the swollen lips of her sex.

Fire raced through her veins and her knees weakened.

"This," his voice grew hoarser now. "I wanted to know how wet I made you."

He pushed a finger between the folds and inside her.

"Hell." His mouth grazed the side of her neck as he pushed the finger deep and began to slowly penetrate her with it. "You're soaked for me."

She bit her lip, not so far gone that she would admit the words aloud.

"Allie. My Allie-cat. My seductive little kitten." He curled his finger, moving it along the wall of her channel. He hit an ultra sensitive spot and she gasped. "Admit you want me."

"The hell I do." She moved against his hand.

"Really?" He pulled his finger from her and she cried out at the loss of sensation. "Well, we'll just have to see about that."

He cupped her ass and lifted her, carrying her over to the bed before he dropped her down. She bounced once and scrambled to sit up.

Going to his knees in front of her, he grabbed her legs and pulled her to the edge.

"You don't want me?"

"No," she lied. The breath locked in her throat as he trailed his fingers up her calves.

"Not even a little bit?" He pushed her dress up around her waist again and bracketed her hips with his hands.

"Not even—" she gasped when he dropped a kiss on the silky fabric still covering her mound, "—a little bit."

"Hmm." His tongue traced her slit through her thong. Up and down. The pressure and wetness of his mouth alone almost made her come.

Tension coiled hot in her belly and the walls of her sex clenched in anticipation.

"I'm not sure I believe you, kitten." He hooked his fingers into the sides of her thong and tugged it off her hips. The tiny scrap of material slid down her body and off.

Oh God, it was insane how bad she wanted his mouth on her. She clenched her fists and stared down at Clint kneeling between her thighs.

He gave the slightest smile as he studied her swollen sex. Almost like he was forming a plan of attack.

His breathing grew heavier as he gripped her calves and lifted her legs over his shoulders. He kissed the inside of her thigh, then caught the sensitive skin between his teeth lightly.

Allison leaned back onto her elbows, pushing herself closer to his mouth. She wouldn't be the one to lose control.

He raised his gaze to hers.

Without looking away, he pushed his tongue inside her and despite her vow, she was lost.

Chapter Four

Clint savored the sensual taste of Allie in his mouth, but even more, the uninhibited cry she made while he teased her.

She'd been leaning back, seeming so in control and calm. Almost challenging him when he'd gone to his knees in front of her. But the moment he'd buried his face between her legs, it was quite obvious who had control.

Finally. God, how long had he wanted her? Wanted her begging and crying out with pleasure from his touch.

Gripping her ass cheeks, he moved her more snug against his face, pushing his tongue deep inside her.

"Oh God," she gasped, her hips rising and falling off the mattress.

His cock strained against his jeans and he considered undoing his fly, but that would mean letting go of her ass. And God, she had the most amazing ass.

With her cries growing more guttural, he slid his tongue up to find her clit. Thick and swollen, he circled the kernel and ran his tongue over it.

"*Clint.*"

His name on her sweet lips spurred him on, and he drew her clit into his mouth, suckling it and grazing his teeth lightly across it.

When her bottom clenched in his hands, he slowed the caress with his mouth again. He wanted to stretch out her pleasure, build up the climax.

He released her clit from his mouth and started the slow circles with his tongue again. Keeping his gaze on her stomach and breasts, he watched them rise and fall in jerky movements with each ragged breath she took.

Her thighs tightened around his head and he knew she was going to come. He latched on to the sensitive button again and sucked hard, pulling her over the edge.

She cried out and her elbows slid outward as she fell onto her back, her entire body shaking through the orgasm.

He stayed with her, gentling how hard he sucked her. Trailing his tongue over the bud, light and teasing to ease her down from her peak.

Only when she went limp on the bed, her legs dead weight over his shoulders, did he pull away.

"Interesting response," he murmured, lowering her legs to the bed, "for someone who says they don't want me."

Allison gave a weak snort and rolled over onto her stomach, the round globes of her ass now waving prominently in his face.

"And what are you going to do about it?"

Shit. His gaze locked on the swollen, creamy folds just barely showing below her ass. He hardened even further and he ground his teeth together.

What he wanted to do was pull her onto her knees, unzip his jeans and plunge into her hot center from behind. But going down on her had been an unexpected—and pleasing—delay from what he had to do.

He glanced at his watch and cursed. Could he trust her? Remembering the way she'd nearly got hit on the highway, he sighed. No. It was probably a little too early to trust that Allison wouldn't run the first chance she got.

This next part would be tricky, and God knew she was going to be spitting mad by the time he was done.

Divert and attack.

He walked to his suitcase and pulled out a necktie—who would have thought he'd need it for reasons other than the wedding?—and tucked it quickly into the back of his jeans.

"What am I going to do about it, kitten?"

Reaching the bed, he crawled across it toward her. He pulled his hand back and gave her bottom a sharp slap.

"*Oh.*" Her cry was one of shock and pleasure. "What was that for?"

"That was for trying to run away." He grabbed her hip and flipped her onto her back, then pulled her body higher up on the bed toward the headboard.

She scooted willingly, the heat and desire in her eyes still blazing as she stared up at him.

"Oh yeah?" She licked her lips and her knees fell open, once again revealing the tempting folds of her still swollen sex.

"Yeah." He knelt between her legs and leaned down to kiss her curved mouth.

Her soft sigh got crushed beneath the force of his lips. *So tempting.* God almighty, it was crazy how much he wanted her. His tongue slipped inside to stroke against hers, while he took her wrists in one hand and forced them above her head.

He reached between them to rub her clit again, listening to her quickly drawn breaths. Knowing she would be slow to react while he was pleasing her, he let go of her wrists to grab the necktie. He quickly wound the tie around her wrists, before using both hands to make a quick knot.

She pulled away, her dazed expression growing more hesitant. "You sure skip right to the kinky part. I never would have thought that about you, Clint."

"Hmm. There's a lot about me you don't know." He secured the other end of the tie to the headboard and gave it a tug, making sure there was no leeway. "But you'll have to find all that out later."

"Later?" she repeated huskily. "Then why are you tying me up now?"

"I need to run to the store and pick up some things. The stores close in a half hour." He nibbled on her bottom lip. "And I don't want to lose time worrying about you running off again."

"What?" Her eyes bugged and her mouth flapped.

"I'll make it up to you," he promised with a wink, then slid down her body to nuzzle the sweetness between her legs one last time.

Her thighs slammed around his head, squeezing his ears in a grip that nearly had his eyes crossing.

"Untie me now, Clint, or so help me God I'll break your neck."

Prying her thighs apart he lifted himself away from her, gasping on a laugh.

"That was funny, Allie. You steal that move from a James Bond movie?" He moved to grab his keys off the dresser.

"*What?*" She thrashed against her restraints, her body flipping about the bed like a fish out of water.

He bit his lip to avoid laughing, somehow he knew she wouldn't appreciate it. "I'll be back before you know it."

"Clint, you son of a bitch—"

"Sorry, kitten. Don't hate me too much." He reached the door and with a quick wave, disappeared.

After twenty minutes—and she knew from staring at the clock on the wall—Allison gave up trying to get free and went limp on the bed.

She had better ways to spend her energy—like plotting the medieval-style torture she would inflict on Clint the first chance she got.

Humiliation still burned in every inch of her body. How could she have been so stupid? To allow him to nearly seduce her and, worse yet, to have *enjoyed* it. Hell, enjoy was an understatement. That had been, simply and put in an obvious cliché, mind blowing.

Sure, being tied up and ravished had always been one of her fantasies, but seeing as he'd skipped the ravished part, the fantasy kind of died.

And Clint was probably still laughing all the way down the fluorescent-lit aisles of the local Walmart.

When he'd touched her she'd lost all rationale. Had only been focused on the intensity of pleasure she'd never really experienced before today when she was intimate with a man.

Just the memory of what had happened between them had her body aching with the need to be filled by him. She pressed her thighs together to ease the sensation.

Bastard. What was the one thing she could do to regain control? To humiliate him as much as he had her? Tell him his dick was small?

She sighed and closed her eyes. Yeah, like that would work, because it obviously wasn't true. She'd always suspected Clint was well endowed and now she knew for sure.

When he'd been pressed up against her on the side of the road, she'd felt him. Felt the thick curl of his erection against her belly, and the memory was branded in her mind and body.

But she couldn't let herself give in again. If he returned and tried to touch her, she'd fight him this time. Fight him and her annoying hormones.

Calm down. You need to calm down. She groaned and closed her eyes. Time to do some meditative breathing. Hopefully that would help.

Breathe in. Breathe out. Relax. Focus only on the breathing. She repeated the process, feeling a familiar calm slip over her.

Her jaw popped with a yawn, but she kept breathing. In and out. In and out. In and out...

Clint left the store with a giant plastic bag gripped in his hands. He scowled, casting an uneasy glance over his shoulder back into the store.

Lord what kind of hell had that been? He'd spent too much time flipping through clothes and underwear racks. Searching to find just the right size. Shopping was what some people might call it. Women actually enjoyed this? Talk about a nightmare.

He shuddered and thrust a hand through his hair, heading toward his SUV. Unlocking the door, he tossed the bag onto the passenger seat and climbed behind the wheel. His stomach growled and he rubbed his hand across it.

Allison had another reason to be mad at him. He'd promised her food then left her alone, tied up in the motel room. Guilt pricked in his gut and he sighed, somewhat regretting his impulsive decision to lock her up. He'd deserved her anger.

He drove down the highway until he spotted the one and only restaurant still open. A fast-food burger joint. Somehow he couldn't imagine Allison getting excited about a burger, but if she were hungry enough, he'd wager she'd eat it.

Turning into the drive-thru he bought a few cheeseburgers, a couple of orders of fries and a big root beer they could both sip on.

Pulling into the motel parking lot, he half expected to find the door to their room wide open and Allison long gone. He wouldn't put it past her to have found a way out of his tie.

But the door was still shut. He narrowed his eyes and put the SUV into park.

Taking a deep breath in, he prepped himself to get the cursing of his life. He climbed out of the vehicle and headed for the room, inserting the key and then pushing it open an inch.

Silence. No screams or sounds of the bed squeaking as she fought to get free.

After pushing the door open all the way, his glance landed on the bed. She'd fallen asleep.

Clint dropped the bag onto the floor and closed the door behind him. He walked quietly over to the bed and sat on the edge.

Her brows were drawn together, her mouth curved down into a frown. Even while sleeping she was pissed at him. Well, he didn't blame her. With a soft smile, he touched her cheek with the tips of his fingers.

Allison groaned and stirred, but still didn't open her eyes.

Clint reached for the headboard and unfastened the tie, freeing her wrists and laying them at her side. She immediately curled up into a ball.

He pulled back the bedspread on one side, then lifted her enough to set her gently on the sheets, covering her again with the blankets.

Her eyelids fluttered open, but her gaze was unfocused and still full of sleep.

"What a shitty dream," she mumbled, before her eyes closed again.

Amusement lanced through him, and he laughed silently. For the briefest moment, he'd considered waking her up to make her eat dinner, because she had to be hungry. But watching her drag the blankets to her chin and wiggle her head against the pillow with a sigh, he thought better of it. She could eat later.

He went back to the bag of food and pulled out his own portion of dinner. After devouring the burger in a few bites he went on to the fries. The entire time he ate, he watched her.

She looked a little too innocent. Seeing her like this would make someone doubt that she could nearly spit fire when mad and curse until she was blue in the face. No. Sleeping Allison looked like she spent her days hanging out on the Martha Stewart show. Made him think of how Allie had used to be.

He set the extra burger and fries in the fridge before grabbing his duffle bag and heading off to the bathroom.

Ten minutes later he came out, teeth clean and ready for bed. They would be heading out early in the morning, and he suspected they wouldn't be getting as much sleep the rest of the week.

He climbed into the other side of the bed and slipped beneath the blankets. The heat from Allison's body radiated across the few inches separating them. The floral scent of her perfume tickled his nostrils, and he took a deep breath in, savoring it.

His body stirred and he bit back a groan. *There's no reason to touch her. Absolutely none.*

Ignoring the rational side of his brain, he scooted closer and draped an arm over her waist. He yawned, closed his eyes and waited for sleep.

The growling of her stomach woke her. Then the realization she was snuggled up against a body, a hard, warm, man-smelling body.

Was she still dreaming? Mmm. She smiled and snuggled closer to the warmth. Because there'd been some parts of her dream that had been absolutely delicious.

Wait. There'd also been parts of the dream that had pretty bad...like getting tied up. The smile faded and she blinked open her eyes.

Ack. So not a dream. He was here. Clint Novak was lying in bed with her and had an arm thrown around her waist like they'd just made love.

But then, they had almost done just that. The parts of her "dream" that had been delicious had been when she'd let Clint go down on her.

Oh God. Just thinking about it sent a rush of moisture between her legs, and she clenched her thighs together.

She glanced at the clock on the wall, squinting to see the time since it was still dark. Four-thirty in the morning? Was that right?

Jerking her gaze back to him, she frowned. Why hadn't he wakened her? His mouth twitched and he released a small snore.

Careful to not move the mattress too much, she slid out from under his arm and moved off the bed. Once she realized she'd gotten out of bed without waking him, she let out a quick breath.

Her stomach growled again and she slapped her palm over it, willing it to shut up. Fortunately he'd left her almost fully dressed—she wasn't about to search for her thong. All the better to get the hell out of here.

She held her breath as she tip-toed toward the door. Her hand closed over the cold knob of the door handle.

The light turned on. "Going to get us breakfast, kitten?"

Son of a *bitch*. She closed her eyes and fisted her hands.

"Could you, maybe, pass out again so I can sneak away with some success?"

Clint laughed, which turned into a yawn. "Not on your life. Come back to bed."

"I'm hungry."

"Mmm. Check the mini fridge."

She narrowed her eyes, giving him a wary glance as she crossed the room toward the small fridge. He'd picked up some food? Maybe yogurt, or bagels and cream cheese... she tugged open the fridge and her expression fell.

Lifting the bag out with one finger, she wrinkled her nose. "Is this what I think it is?"

"Well, it has the words *Happy Burger* on the bag, what do you think it is?"

His sarcasm did little for her growing annoyance. She gritted her teeth and opened the paper bag, staring down at the cold fries and burger.

"You've got to be kidding me." She sighed. "Clint, I don't even eat this shit hot. And now you want me to suck it down cold?"

He propped himself up in bed, leaning on one elbow as a devilish gleam lit his eyes.

"Well, I guess I know something else you could suck down if you really want to."

Her mouth fell open and she could feel her cheeks heating.

"The cold burger suddenly sounds fabulous," she choked out instead.

She unwrapped the burger and glared at him, before turning her frustration to the food. Lifting it to her mouth, she closed her eyes and hoped it didn't come right back up. Her stomach welcomed the meal, as odd as it might've been at four in the morning.

"Atta girl, flashback to those drunken midnight burger runs in college."

She swallowed her bite, then gave him a tight smile. "I didn't have any drunken burger runs in college. And you shouldn't be driving drunk anyway."

"I didn't. I was generally the designated driver." Clint sighed. "You used to have so much fun, Allie. Got a little wild, a little dirty, what happened to you?"

"What happened? I got serious about life. We can't all keep traipsing through the mud chasing butterflies our whole lives." She rolled her eyes then took another bite, swallowing a moment later. "Or maybe those who become forest rangers can."

His mouth curved into a sleepy, sexy as hell smile. "Something like that, yeah."

Finishing the burger, she threw the trash in the garbage and grabbed the drink stuffed into the fridge. After taking a hefty sip, she placed it back and shut the fridge door.

"You done eating?"

She gave a terse nod and folded her arms across her chest, biting her lip. What now? Surely he wouldn't make her—

"Come back to bed, Allie."

Okay, he would. She swallowed hard.

"It's much too early to get up. Come back to bed."

"I'd rather not." She sniffed. "I think you should consider yourself lucky you got to sleep in there once with me."

"I could always come and get you. Maybe bring out my tie again..."

Her pulse quickened. "You wouldn't dare. You're already on my shit-list for that little stunt."

He arched a brow and swung a leg out of bed.

"Okay, I'm coming," she muttered and strode to the bed with a scowl. "If you're even thinking about—"

"I'm not thinking about anything right now except getting a couple more hours of sleep, Allie."

Her jaw clenched as she climbed beneath the covers next to him.

Clint reached across her to flip the light off again before lying back down. His thigh brushed her hips and she stiffened.

Tingles spread through her body and heat lingered in the small area where their bodies touched. She pulled in a shallow breath and stared in the darkened room at the ceiling.

Clint's breathing, steady and calm, lulled her into a false sense that escape would be all too easy. But she knew better now. She knew the minute she climbed off this bed and ran for the door he'd be on her. And he'd tie her down again.

"Go to sleep."

With a frustrated curse, she rolled away from him onto her side. Scooting as far to the other end of the bed as possible.

Right. Like she'd actually be able to sleep. She closed her eyes and practiced some deep breathing moves again that would at least relax her.

"Do you need your inhaler?"

"What?" Her eyes snapped open.

"You're breathing kind of funny. I just thought you might have developed asthma recently."

"*What?*" Her mouth flapped. "I'm not asthmatic, you freaking idiot, I'm doing breathing exercises."

"Well can you do them in the morning? You're keeping me awake."

This time she made no effort to stifle her growl of frustration.

"Sheath your claws, kitten," Clint murmured and she could hear the smile in his voice. "You can cuss me out when we wake up again."

Allison snapped her eyes closed and her mouth shut. Yes, maybe a few hours sleep more was a good idea. Something told her she would need her energy in the morning.

Chapter Five

Clint closed his eyes, but couldn't fall back asleep. Instead he thought about his plan for the week.

When Allison realized where he was taking her, she'd likely have a bit of a meltdown. Even if fifteen years ago she would've been in her element...

A couple of hours passed and the first rays of sunlight peeked through the gap in the curtains.

Sitting up in bed, he glanced down at Allison again. She'd curled up on her side into fetal position, her back to him.

He climbed out of bed, debating whether to grab a shower while she slept. He hesitated, telling himself she could wake up in minutes and be out the door while he was still washing down Clint Junior.

Oh, well, he'd risk it. Crossing the room to the bathroom, he turned on the shower and left the bathroom door open. With the door open he still had a clear view of the bed.

Still keeping his gaze on her, he jerked his T-shirt over his head and kicked off his boxers. He reached into the shower, found the water warm, then stepped beneath the spray.

He showered in record time, using the toiletries the motel offered. Everything else was packed and he had no intentions of heading out to the SUV to get them.

Shutting off the water, he stepped out into the cool air and grabbed a towel. He wrapped it around his waist and hurried back into the room.

Allison's eyes flicked open the moment he passed by the bed. She scrambled into sitting position.

"You're naked."

"I'm not naked," he chuckled with amusement. "Obviously, since I have a towel around my waist."

She moved her gaze over him, from head to toe. Her cheeks reddened and he watched the muscles in her throat work.

Interesting reaction. He resisted the smug laugh threatening. Allie wanted him, deny it all she wanted. Her blatant appreciative gaze and response to his touch last night only confirmed it.

"We're going to head out soon," he murmured, ruffling through his duffle bag for some clothes. "You may want to grab a shower."

"A shower?" Her gaze danced away from him. "But I don't have my shampoo or curling iron."

"There's hotel shampoo. Besides, it'll be good practice for the week I have planned." He pulled out a clean pair of boxers and, knowing she'd probably freak out and run to the bathroom, dropped the towel. "Now about that shower."

In the process of pulling his boxers on, he heard her choked gasp as she scrambled out of bed and ran to the bathroom. The door slammed shut hard behind her.

A laugh did escape from him this time, and he enjoyed it. He pulled a gray T-shirt from his bag and tugged it over his head, then reached for his jeans.

The shower turned on and he could hear her muttering about cheap motel shampoo. His smile widened. Hell, this stuff would be a luxury compared to what she'd be using by morning.

His stomach rumbled, and he passed a hand across it. They'd have to find food somewhere. A granola bar just wouldn't cut it. They'd already eaten crap for dinner last night.

Watching Allie gnaw on a cold burger in the wee hours of the morning had been almost comical.

He glanced at his watch and scowled. Fifteen minutes already. How long did it take a woman to wash her hair for goodness sake?

"Allison?" He crossed the room and rapped on the door. "You okay in there?"

"Go away. I'll be out in ten."

Another ten? His brows drew together and he bit back a curse. His stomach growled louder.

Jeez. High maintenance women were a pain in the butt. Hence the reason he never dated them.

Admitting defeat for now, he went and packed up their stuff so they'd be ready to go. Once that was complete, he grabbed the bag of clothes he'd purchased last night and pulled out an outfit for her to wear. He'd just laid out the panties when the bathroom door opened.

"What are those?"

The horror in her voice had his gaze jerking up. *Bad idea.* His cock tightened under his jeans and the air hissed from between clenched teeth.

Apparently she'd decided walking around in a towel was fair game. Except the small white cloth barely covered her breasts and showed entirely too much thigh and leg.

He jerked his gaze away and dropped a bra onto the bed. "Your clothes."

"I have clothes."

"You have the clothes you wore yesterday," he pointed out. "You'll be with me for an entire week."

"Yeah, and not by choice might I remind you." She glared at him and pushed wet strand of hair off her face. "I'll wear my dress again. It's much preferable—"

"You're not going to want to wear a dress where we're going, Allie."

She strode forward and scooped the clothes. "What is this, polyester?"

The clean smell of soap and woman tickled his nostrils. He took a quick step backward and fisted his hands so he wouldn't reach out and touch her again.

At her scowl of distaste his jaw tightened and annoyance rippled through him.

"I have no idea if it's polyester. Sorry, didn't quite check the labels for fabric type."

"Yeah, well, maybe you should've."

A sharp laugh escaped his chest, but he wasn't amused. "Has anyone ever told you you're high maintenance?"

"I prefer calling it having standards. And how did you know my size?"

"I guessed. My, you woke up bitchy this morning."

"Really, Clint? Really?" She glared at him. "You expected otherwise? And I'm sure you're wrong on my size. I mean how could..." She looked at the tags and muttered in dismay. Scowling, she spun on her heel, and marched back into the bathroom.

God almighty, but he almost hoped the clothing made her break out in hives. Of course that would mar her damn near flawless skin. Skin so soft against his lips. Skin that—*shit*. He really needed to get a hold of himself.

He checked the room to see if he'd forgotten to pack anything and came up clean.

The door clicked open and he lifted his gaze to the bathroom again. A laugh built up in his chest, but he quickly smothered it at her withering look.

"Could you be any more obvious?" She walked past him, stuffed her clothes from last night into his bag, and then reached for the athletic shoes he'd bought. "Just go ahead and laugh already."

He cleared his throat and scratched the back of his neck. "I'm not laughing. You look..."

"I look like turquoise sausage for Christ's sake." She narrowed her eyes. "Turquoise is not in my color scheme."

Clint shouldered the backpack and grabbed the other bags on the ground. "I don't know, Allie. It looks pretty good to me. Though I'm thinking the daisy on the sweatshirt makes you appear a little sweeter than you are."

"Fuck you," she snarled and stepped past him and out the door he held open.

"I plan on it. And watch your mouth."

"Not a chance to either."

Clint laughed and followed her to his SUV. His gaze lowered to her ass, all too enticing in its feminine swing. Even beneath the plain sweats, the curves of her body were still hard to hide.

She arrived at his vehicle and reached for the handle. Clint slapped his hand on the door and held it shut.

Her body stiffened and she inhaled sharply. A second later she spun around to face him, their bodies brushed.

"And that whole thing last night?" She lifted an eyebrow, her expression perfectly composed. "Let's just say I had some built-up sexual tension and you happened to be around to release it."

It wasn't as easy to keep the slight smile on his face. "Any Tom, Dick or Harry would have done?"

"Well, I prefer dick, but in an urgent situation I've even been known to grab a Bob."

"Bob?"

She tilted her head and gave him a saccharine smile. "Battery operated boyfriend."

The image of Allison on the bed, going wild with a vibrator flashed through his head. The air rushed from between his clenched teeth and his dick hardened beneath his jeans.

"Aah, how cute. Clint Junior's awake with no one to play with." She lowered her gaze pointedly before raising it again and batting her eyelashes. "Can you open my door now, please? Or would you prefer I make another run for the highway."

Clint removed his hand with a low growl and jerked open the door for her. How had she managed to get the upper hand so quickly?

She climbed into the vehicle and pulled the door shut behind her.

He walked back around to the driver's side, scowling as he climbed in and tossed the bag and backpack into the backseat. Not for one moment did he believe she hadn't wanted him as much as he wanted her last night. The chemistry between them nearly made them tear off each other's clothes the minute they got within ten feet of each other.

Lord, this week with her was going to be a pain in the butt in some ways. But in others...it was going to be a pleasure. To have her admit again that she wanted him like there was no tomorrow.

"What's for breakfast?" she asked, plucking at the flower on her shirt. "And don't try to tell me a cold hamburger was my breakfast."

He grunted and started the engine. "It wasn't. We'll stop in town at a diner before we hit the road. It's a long drive."

"Did you buy me a book?"

"What?" He pulled onto the highway and gave her a sideways glance.

"A book. Did you buy me one so I'm not bored?"

"I didn't realize it was my job to entertain you."

"Well you should have, you're my kidnapper." She folded her hands across her lap and glanced out the window. "As you deemed it necessary to abduct me, the least you could have done was see to it that I wouldn't be bored on our *long drive.*"

"Your line of reasoning is a little bit left field."

"Says the man who kidnapped me."

"Look, will you stop using that word?"

"Will you take me back to Seattle?"

Clint sighed and shook his head, frustrated and yet a little amused by the conversation.

"Then it's a kidnapping," she murmured in a singsong tone.

"Look, we can stop at a drugstore if you really want a book."

"Really?" Her voice rose. "Ah, thanks, Clint."

"You're welcome."

He scratched the back of his neck and cast a nervous glance her way, a little uneasy by her light, verbal sparring. She was probably just trying to keep him off balance. And she was succeeding.

Reaching for the stereo, he turned on the music and relaxed as a country song filtered into the vehicle through the speakers.

"Jeez, please don't tell me we're going to have to listen to this cowboy stuff the entire time."

His chest swelled with the slow breath he drew in. At least she'd dropped the perkiness. Argumentative and cursing Allie he'd grown used to. Could even deal with.

He reached forward and twisted the volume up another notch, his lips twitching.

"God," she groaned. "It sounds like somebody's gutting a cow."

"That's no cow, that's Tim McGraw."

"Well, he sounds like a cow getting his innards ripped out."

His mouth tightened. God, how could he lust after a woman who thought Tim McGraw sounded like a dying cow?

"Well, country stations are about all we get out here anyway."

She sighed. "If you'd have told me you were going to kidnap me, I could have brought some of my CDs."

"Told you? Kidnapping's don't work that—damn, Allie!" He slammed his hand on the dashboard. "Are you trying to drive me nuts?"

"Yes. Is it working? Ready to take me home yet?"

"Yes, to the first. And no to the second."

"Good, to the first and you'll regret it to the second." She sighed. "How far until we reach the diner?"

"Just a couple of minutes." Hopefully he could make it that long. A feisty Allison and a growling stomach were not a good combination this early in the morning.

"Good, I'm starving. I hope they have awesome coffee."

"Coffee is coffee. It's all the same."

"Oh. God. Surely it hasn't been *that* long since you visited Seattle." She glanced over at him again.

"If you recall, I'm from Montana."

"Right." She nodded. "So Montana is the only place for you?"

"Wouldn't live anywhere else. Born and raised there."

Allison leaned back in her seat and watched his face transform the moment he mentioned Montana. Clint was a man who loved his home. When he thought about it the tension visibly eased from his shoulders and his mouth curled upward, the hint of laugh lines appeared in the corners of his eyes.

Montana sounded like too much land and not enough shopping malls in her opinion—though she'd never been. Definitely not her cup of tea. But then again, the mind-numbing traffic of the city had made her consider moving out of town recently. Country life might sound a bit hairy, but it also had its appeal.

Her friend, Christy, who used to work at the same school in Seattle with her, had recently moved out to the country and apparently loved the slower pace of life. Of course the fact that she'd met and eventually married a sexy cowboy had a lot to do with that.

Allison folded her arms across her chest and drew in a deep breath. While getting dressed this morning she'd made the decision to try and be a little less hostile. This was Clint and despite their current circumstances, they were originally friends. And maybe if she was nice for awhile she'd be able to convince him that she wasn't after getting Kenneth back like Clint seemed to be convinced.

"Here we are."

The vehicle bounced into the gravel parking lot before coming to a stop out front of the small diner.

Allison reached for the door handle, but he leaned over and caught her wrist. She looked at her wrist, then lifted her gaze to his.

"Promise me you'll behave yourself."

She arched an eyebrow. "Are you afraid I'll beat my chest and throw my eggs at the locals or something?"

"Of course not." He held her gaze, and she saw the wariness there. "I just don't want you running onto the highway or trying to tell someone in the restaurant I kidnapped you."

She blinked and looked away, having had no intention to do such a thing. Right now all she wanted was food. Real food.

"Allison?" His voice deepened. "I don't want to have to worry about it. Otherwise we can just keep going and hit a drive-thru later."

"Oh God, no. No more fast food." She shook her head and sighed. "I promise. I'll behave myself. Girl Scouts honor."

His lips twitched. "I don't recall you ever being a Girl Scout."

"You're right. I wasn't." She shuddered. "I'm so not a camper."

"I don't know. There was a time you didn't mind getting a little dirt under your nails." He gave her a considering look.

"Yeah, that time was before I came to my senses." Allison wrinkled her nose and climbed out of the SUV, her new shoes crunching on the rocks. She followed Clint toward the front door and glanced down at her feet, analyzing the sturdy shoes he'd picked out for her.

The man must have been on a mission at the store last night. Panties, clothes, bras, socks and even these fashion challenged shoes. Although most things he'd bought had seemed practical, she'd noted all the underwear were thongs. No granny panties in sight. And even one of the two bras had been sexy, the other had been a sports bra.

Clint pulled open the door to the restaurant and gestured for her to go in first.

"Howdy, folks, grab any booth available." A harried waitress scurried by them, barely glancing their way as she went to take an order at another table.

Allison made her way to an empty booth, saliva pooling in her mouth at the smell of bacon, eggs and syrup. She slid onto the plastic seat and folded her hands on the table.

Instead of sitting across from her as she'd expected, Clint came to her side of the table and sat down. She scooted further into the booth, right up next to the window. But the booth was too small to put any real distance between them.

His denim clad thigh rubbed against hers, sending spirals of heat through her and her pulse into overdrive.

Chapter Six

"Is there a reason you need to sit right next to me?" she asked lightly.

"Oh you know. Just want to make sure you don't throw any eggs."

She smothered a laugh and shook her head.

Two menus sailed across the table, followed by a perky, "Hey there, folks. I'm your waitress, Bernice."

"Hello," Allie and Clint said in unison.

"The breakfast special today is biscuits and gravy, a sausage patty and hashbrowns. We don't take checks unless you're local. Can I get either of you a cup of coffee?" The entire spiel came out on one breath.

"Yes, please." Allison glanced up and offered a faint smile to the waitress, who appeared to be pushing seventy.

"I'll take some too." Clint turned the coffee mug in front of him right-side up, then reached for Allison's to do the same.

The waitress nodded and leaned over to fill both mugs.

"You folks need a moment with the menu?"

"Just a few if you don't mind, Bernice." Clint's broad smile charmed the hurry out of the older woman.

She flushed and tucked a strand of gray hair behind her ear.

"Oh, well you two just take your time. I'll be back around in a few."

Allison reached for her mug of coffee and lifted it to her mouth, blowing on the steaming drink.

"You don't like camping anymore?"

She turned her head slightly to look at him. "I prefer a nice hotel." Pursing her lips, she blew again on her coffee. "Why do you ask?"

He picked up his own coffee with a shrug. "Just curious I guess."

Hmm. She narrowed her eyes and took a sip. Definitely not Ooo La Latté, but it'd do.

"How is it?"

"It'll work." She set the mug down and grabbed the menu again.

She scanned her options and it only took a moment to find what she was looking for. Shutting her menu again, she tossed it back down on the table.

"What are you getting?"

"The farmer's omelet."

"Huh." His brows lifted and his lower lip jutted forward in a manner entirely too sensual. "Good to see you still like your meat."

"I like protein. It's how I keep my girlish figure."

Clint laughed and shook his head. "You've got a great figure. Keep eating your protein."

Biting back a snort, she decided not to remind him that by society standards she could stand to lose fifteen pounds.

The waitress returned and grinned down at them. "Ready?"

"We sure are. We'll both get the farmer's omelet."

Allison, having opened her mouth to order, closed it again.

Bernice nodded and scribbled on her pad. "Great. Toast and hashbrowns or pancakes for you both?"

"Toast and hashbrowns," Clint said before she could speak again.

"For you both?"

"Yes." He glanced at her. "Or do you prefer pancakes now?"

Oh God she wanted to say pancakes just to be difficult, but damn it she didn't want them. It irritated her he remembered what she liked to eat.

She finally smiled. "Toast and hashbrowns is great. Thanks."

"All right, kids." Bernice closed her note pad and gave them a cheery smile. "That'll be up for you shortly."

The older woman walked off and left them alone again. Allison glanced out the window and stared at the miles of empty land only intersected by the highway.

"Do you come here ever? Over the mountains?"

Her mouth twitched at his question. "Actually I do, or used to. I had a lot of friends who went to college in Pullman."

"Is that so?"

"Mmm hmm."

"Think you could ever live anywhere besides Seattle?"

"I don't know...I'm sure if I had a reason." She took another sip of coffee. Where was he going with this line of questioning? "Would you ever consider moving to the Seattle area?"

He lowered his gaze to her mouth and she watched the heat flicker in his eyes. Her pulse jumped and she inhaled sharply and pulled back, distancing herself from him again. Well, as much as the small booth allowed.

"It'd take a lot to convince me."

Hmm. And what could *a lot* mean? Not that it really mattered... Clint wasn't a city guy. He didn't fit any more in the city than she did out of it.

They sat in silence for a bit, both lost in their own thoughts.

"Here you are, kids." Bernice reappeared, two massive plates in her hands.

"Good God that's a lot of food." Allison watched as the waitress set down one plate in front of her.

"Well, we get a lot of truckers through here." She winked. "We believe in filling up the bellies."

"I'm almost full just looking at it." Allison pulled the napkin onto her lap and reached for her fork. "Thank you."

"Anything else I can get you folks?"

"Ketchup," she and Clint said the same time.

Allison grimaced. Jesus, they had cloned appetites.

"You've got it." Bernice reached behind her and grabbed a bottle off the empty table across the way. "Enjoy your breakfast and I'll be back with some more coffee in a bit."

Clint handed her the ketchup and she didn't miss the twitching of his lips.

She squirted a hefty dose of ketchup onto her hashbrowns, then set the bottle back down in front of him.

"We probably could have split one of these omelets," Clint remarked.

Allison snorted and glanced at his plate. "Speak for yourself. I'm hungry. Some of us went to bed—or sorry, got tied to the bed—without dinner last night."

Clint's gaze darted around the restaurant and she caught a faint flush stealing up his neck. She couldn't resist a small laugh.

"Ah, what's the matter, Clint? Don't want the locals to know about your kinky habits?"

"Allie, hush up and eat your omelet already," he hissed and tucked into his own breakfast.

Her laughter grew. She lifted the fork to her mouth and her stomach rumbled loudly the moment the food touched her lips.

All thoughts faded as she went to work appeasing her appetite. Despite her intent of eating her entire omelet, she barely made it to the halfway point. With a pained groan, she pushed the plate aside and grabbed her last piece of toast.

"Told you we should have split it."

She glanced at his plate and snorted. "You ate your entire omelet."

"Only because it was there." He set his napkin down and downed the rest of his coffee. "Besides, I'm not sure when we'll get to eat next. It could be granola bars for awhile."

She wrinkled her nose. "Where are we going?"

"East."

Chomping into her toast she gave him a sarcastic smile. "Very helpful, thank you. You're a real pro at giving ambiguous answers."

"Thank you. I need to use the bathroom."

"Are you asking my permission?"

He met her gaze. "No. I'm warning you to beha—"

"Behave? Right. How could I forget?" She rubbed her stomach and leaned back in the booth. "Go on now. I won't run into oncoming traffic."

He lifted an eyebrow. "Or beg the locals for help?"

"Not even that."

"All right. I'll be back in a few."

"Okay." The breath caught in her throat as she watched him walk away from her.

She was free. If she wanted to, she could run right on out that door...into the middle of nowhere. If only she had her phone. She glanced outside at his SUV and her pulse jumped.

Her phone was in her purse. And her purse was in his vehicle.

Before she could let herself feel guilty—because she had *nothing* to feel guilty about—she slid from the booth and hurried out the front door of the restaurant. Her feet pounded on the loose rocks as she sprinted to the SUV.

Please be unlocked. Please.

Her fingers wrapped around the handle and she jerked. The door swung open. *Yes.* She climbed in and slammed the locks shut on all the doors.

"This is what happens, Clint, when you don't lock your doors. The city is good for something," she said aloud and dove for her purse.

The cell phone was at the bottom, but before she'd even pulled it free from her purse she'd hit speed dial and was calling Leah.

"Good Lord it's early," her friend answered a minute later.

"Leah! Damn, I'm in a mess. You've gotta help me."

"What? Allison, what's going on? Did you talk to Kenneth yesterday?"

"No," her gaze jerked up as she saw movement outside the door. "Ack!"

Clint's palm slapped against the window and she jumped back with a yelp.

"Look, Leah, I've been kidnapped. Sort of, not really. I mean, I don't want you to call the police or anything."

"Kidnapped?" Leah's voice rose. "By who? Allison, what's going on?"

Clint jammed his key into the door and she lurched forward to hold down the lock.

"Damn it, Allison," he growled and twisted harder.

"Go ahead, break your damn key, Clint," she taunted. "You're not getting back in here."

"Allison?" Leah prodded from the other end of the line. "Who's Clint? Not Clint Novak is it? Where are you?"

Despite her attempts to keep him out, the lock popped up. She shrieked and dove for the backseat.

Clint jerked open the door and dove into the SUV after her. He caught her ankle right as she landed on the backseat.

"Argh, let go of my foot, you idiot!"

Clint's body landed on top of hers and she gasped, arching away from him.

He ripped the phone from her grasp, then the weight of his body lifted from hers.

"Hello, Leah, is it?" he asked, gripping the phone to his ear. "It's Clint. Yes, Clint Novak. I remember you too. How've you been?"

Allison's eyes widened and she grabbed his wrist. "Hey, give me that back. That is *my* phone and *my* friend."

He put a hand against her shoulder, holding her a safe distance from him.

"Right. No...no she's telling the truth, actually. I did kidnap her."

"See? I told you," Allison yelled. "And I changed my mind, call the police, Leah!"

"Right, well, here's the reason," Clint went on. "I'm getting the impression Allison wants to break up his wedding next week...ah, you too? So you knew about it." He nodded. "Uh huh. Right, yes those were my thoughts as well."

"*What*?" Her eyes bugged.

"I'll only keep her for the week...oh would you? Thanks, Leah, that would be great." He nodded. "I appreciate your understanding. I'll have her back by Monday."

"Leah, you can't be serious!" Allison screamed.

"Yes, I'll make it just like a little vacation for her." He turned and gave her a hard smile. "Okay, Leah, have a good time at your step class. Take care now."

He closed the phone and his smile disappeared.

"Oh my God. You did not..." she took a deep breath, rage pounding through her blood. "Did not just get *my best friend* on your side."

"Actually, I did." His jaw flexed. "Buckle up. We're leaving."

"I can't believe this. I can*not* believe this," she snapped in exasperation and fumbled for her seatbelt. "How dare you—?"

"Thank you, Allison." He jammed his key into the ignition and started the car.

"Thank you?"

"Yes. Thank you."

"Why?" She eyed him warily, fastening her own seatbelt.

"For the reminder that I can't trust you." He started the engine and backed out of the parking spot.

Guilt pricked lightly in her gut. Why she should feel guilty when he'd been the one to kidnap her made absolutely no sense. But it was there nonetheless. And before she could stop, she was defending herself.

"I promised not to talk to the locals or run for the highway," she muttered. "You never said anything about using the phone."

The look he turned on her was pure disgust. "I shouldn't have had to."

"Well what do you expect, Clint?" she demanded. "I don't *want* to be here. I'm not the type to sit all docile like while I'm being kidnapped."

He gave a short grunt.

"What did Leah say to you?"

He made no response, but kept his gaze on the highway stretched out before them.

"Clint?"

"She gave me her blessing. Said it was a great idea that I took you away for the week." He glanced over at her. "She's worried you still have feelings for Kenneth."

Allison's mouth flapped. "She did not say any of that."

"She did." He held her gaze a second longer before turning back to the road. "And she agreed to tell anyone who asks that you're staying with her for the time being."

Her stomach sank with that last sentence. And there it was in black and white. The green light for her disappearance for an entire week. Not even her best friend would be looking out for her now.

She closed her eyes, the breakfast she'd just eaten swirling heavy in her stomach.

"I can't believe this," she mumbled. "This is just too much."

He didn't reply and the growing silence between them sent a stab of unease through her.

"Will you at least tell me where you're taking me, Clint?"

He gave soft grunt and shifted gear on the SUV. "We're going to Montana."

Clint rubbed a hand across the stubble on his jaw and glanced back at Allison. She was still asleep. Thank God. After hours of listening to her rant and curse—not to mention dodging the granola bars she chucked at him, she'd finally passed out.

Like a toddler after a tantrum. His lips twitched. He glanced at the clock on the dashboard and gave a grunt of approval. They were making excellent time and should arrive within the hour.

He winced and gave a hefty sigh. Her reaction to the Montana news had been bad enough. He didn't look forward to her reaction when she realized their new accommodations. Or lack thereof. The hotel from last night would be a luxury compared to where they were heading next.

I'm so not a camper. Maybe Allie wasn't a camper, but she certainly would be by the time the week was up.

He slowed the SUV to around twenty miles per hour, easing them gently over the small back road leading them deeper into the forest and toward the lake.

The constant bouncing of the vehicle must have jostled Allison awake, because he heard her groan and shift on the seat.

"Ouch. I have the worst crick in my neck."

"You probably slept on it wrong." He glanced in the rearview mirror at her.

"Yeah," she scowled. "Because it's so easy to sleep right in a car."

Grouchy, was she? His mouth thinned as he focused his gaze back on the road.

She gasped. "Oh my God. Where the hell are we? There're trees. *Everywhere*."

"Welcome to Glacier National Park."

"Why are we in a national park?" Her voice squeaked. "Are you taking me on a picnic or something?"

"No. I'm taking you camping."

Chapter Seven

Dead silence met his calm statement. He held his breath and slunk a bit lower in the seat, anticipating another granola bar aimed at his head.

He lifted his gaze to the rearview to catch a glimpse of her reaction. Her eyes had widened to half dollar size, her mouth hung slack.

"No," she finally choked hoarsely. "Did you miss that whole part where I said I didn't camp?"

"It'll be good for you."

"Look you may be a God damn forest ranger, but I am a girl who needs a toilet that flushes."

"Trust me, after a few days of using a pit toilet you'll be a pro."

The scream she let out should have broken the windows in his SUV.

"No. Oh my God, *no*." She unbuckled her seatbelt and reached for the door handle.

"The child locks are on back there now," he said. "Not like it would matter anyway. It's a long walk back to the main road. And an even longer one to any form of civilization."

He slowed the vehicle and turned into the campsite he'd used many times before.

"We're here anyway." He turned off the engine and climbed out of the SUV.

The familiar smell of clean, crisp air and earth hit him and he inhaled deeply, closing his eyes. Montana. Every time he came back from a trip to the city he always wondered how he could ever leave it. This was home.

He glanced in the back of the vehicle. Allison sat stock still, eyes still wide as she stared out the window.

His mouth curved into a smile. And she'd been all too eager to get out of the car just a minute ago.

Walking slowly around to her side, he pulled open the door. "Come on out and get some fresh air."

"The air in here is fine."

"Trust me, it's even better out here." His grin widened. "Besides, I could use your help pitching a tent."

Her head swiveled to him. "Oh no. If you want to pitch a tent, then you do it yourself. I want nothing to do with you or your tent pitching."

He strode forward and grabbed her hand, tugging her out of his vehicle. "Think of it as an adventure."

"It's been an adventure since you kidnapped me yesterday morning."

Relieved that she didn't resist and had stepped outside, he didn't immediately let go of her hand. She didn't seem in any hurry to release his anyway. In fact her grip tightened as her glance darted around the campsite.

The blood moved a little faster through his veins as he breathed in the scent of her. Her perfume from yesterday was gone—washed off in the shower this morning no doubt, and with nothing but soap to replace it. But her scent, the smell of Allison was still there. And God help him, being this close to her nearly set his blood on fire. Sitting next to her at breakfast had been a trial in itself.

"It's so...isolated," she whispered.

"Yes. That's why I love it."

"And you want me to sleep in a...a tent?"

"Yes." He squeezed her hand. "You've done it before, Allie."

"When I was like eight!"

"Right. I considered the fact you might be a bit out of practice and brought the big tent and a blow-up bed."

"Two blow-up beds."

"One. This isn't a negotiation, Allie. It is what it is." He released her hand and moved to open the back of his SUV. "We should set up camp before the sun goes down."

"Oh God. This isn't happening. This can't be happening." She whimpered. "What kind of person kidnaps you and takes you camping? Oh, wait, a forest ranger. God, it's like a bad joke."

A laugh rumbled in his chest as he pulled the tent from the back of the SUV and set it on the ground.

"Is that a *boat* on top of your car?"

"Canoe. Picked it up at my place on the way here. You were sleeping. You slept hard, didn't wake during any of my stops," he answered and gestured to the tent. "Could you set this over in the clearing?"

He didn't check to see if she'd obey—he knew she would—and kept unloading everything.

When he glanced up again, sure enough, she'd hauled the tent over to the clearing near the lake. She straightened and wiped her hands on her sweat pants.

The curves of her body were all too enticing against the backdrop of the glittering blue lake. Her hair lifted in the faint breeze and she looked around, her eyes wide and vulnerable as she worried her bottom lip with her teeth.

So beautiful. Both Allison and the landscape. It should've seemed weird, Allie shadowed in the lush forest of brown trunks and dense green branches. But it wasn't weird. She looked entirely too natural here—whether it made sense or not.

Though she might *look* natural here, Clint reminded himself it might be awhile before she felt at ease. His lips twitched in amusement.

He adjusted the box in his grasp and crossed the site toward her.

"All right. Lesson one," he murmured. "We get that tent up."

"You make it sound so dirty," she grumbled.

"No, your dirty mind makes it sound dirty." He dropped the box on the ground and closed the distance between them.

His hands slid to her hips, pulling her body snug against his.

"But if you want to be dirty—" his voice dropped and his mouth curved into a smile, "—then I have absolutely no problem indulging you."

He felt the tremble that racked her body and saw the flare of matching desire in her gaze.

But her words contrasted her body's response. "I don't want you touching me."

"Don't you?" He lowered his head, his mouth just a breath away from her lips.

"No." Her tongue darted out to moisten, then disappeared again.

"I just don't buy that, kitten." His mouth dropped that tiny distance to claim hers.

Chapter Eight

Soft and damp, her lips parted on a gasp that seemed to be a mix of both annoyance and arousal.

He slipped his tongue into the moist cavern of her mouth, searching the interior for her tongue. He found it, rubbed across the tip in a slow glide of friction and heat.

She made the slightest whimper and tensed, before her body molded into his and her arms slid around his waist.

With a possessive growl, he delved a hand into her hair and held her still so he could deepen the kiss. His cock tightened against his jeans, the need to bury himself inside her took the air from his lungs.

He worked his free hand into the waistband of her sweats and sought the string of the thong panties he'd bought her. Bingo. He snapped the tiny string, a smile curving his lips. She'd worn it.

Moving his hand lower, he palmed her mound, felt the heat and slight dampness there.

She drew in a sharp breath and arched against his hand.

Curling his thumb around the thin panty, he tugged it to the side to expose her.

He used his middle finger to trace her cleft. To play with the hot moisture he found there. God, it was like he *had* to feel it. Find how hot he made her. The knowledge that *he* made her this wet sent a thrill of pure male triumph through him.

"Damn, kitten," he muttered against her mouth. "You have the sweetest body."

He slid his finger deep on the last word.

"*Oh.*" Her cry echoed in the woods as her body clenched around his finger.

God, he wanted Allie like he'd never wanted another woman before. And he'd have her. But unfortunately not right now. Not if they were going to get the campsite set up before nightfall.

He eased back an inch from her and drew in a ragged breath, staring down at her closed eyes and parted lips. His finger still inside her, he drew it up to circle her clit.

Tonight, only after he went down on her until she couldn't think straight again, he'd have her. They'd already waited about six years too long.

The sooner they slept together, the sooner he got over this ridiculous urge to make her his. To claim her on some deep, primitive level.

"We need to set up the tent before the sun sets," he said reluctantly and pulled his finger from her body.

Her body tensed against his and she set her palms against his chest, pushing herself away from him.

"You need to stop that," she muttered.

"Stop what?" he asked, willing his dick to settle down again.

He grabbed the bag the tent was in and opened it up, pulling out the parts.

"Kissing me. Touching me. I told you not to, and I get a little stupid every time you do it."

He laughed and handed her one end of the tent. "A little stupid?" He liked how she admitted it.

"You know what I mean." Obviously flustered, she grabbed the tent and walked backward.

"Go ahead and set it down there."

She dropped her section and fisted her hands against her hips. "Now what?"

"Grab one of those collapsible poles, we need to put them together. Then find the longest one you can find."

She walked over to the pile and sifted through them, finally carrying one back in a way that reminded him of someone pole vaulting.

"This doesn't hold up the tent does it?" she asked with a frown.

"That and a few other poles."

"Hmm. I thought you said you brought the big tent. This sure doesn't look very big."

"Wait until the poles are in it." He winked and inserted the first pole into the necessary loops.

Amazingly enough, she helped him set up the entire thing without complaining; even seemed to get excited to watch the big pile of canvas turn into a raised shelter that would be their home for awhile.

"What now?" she asked, hands on her hips as she eyed the tent.

"Now we set up the inside." He walked back to the SUV and unloaded the last few boxes. "You up to inflating the bed? It shouldn't be too hard."

She snorted and grabbed the box with the picture of the bed on it. "I'm sure."

He watched in amusement as she stumbled to the tent and fumbled around to find how to open the door.

"There's a zipper at the bottom," he finally said.

"Thank you." She scowled and knelt down, finding the tab and jerking it upward.

The door flap fell inward and she climbed into the tent.

"Hmm. It's bigger in here than I thought."

"You haven't blown up the bed yet."

"Hello, patient much? I'm getting to that part."

With a soft laugh, he left her with the project and began to unpack some of the boxes. Thankfully, after his house, he'd also stopped at the grocery before they'd gotten too deep into the woods.

The sound of the air blower came and he glanced toward the tent. Obviously she'd figured out how to blow up the bed.

She emerged from the tent about ten minutes later, a proud smile on her face.

"I did it. The bed's up."

"Good job." He grinned and set out the food they'd eat for dinner, then went and locked the rest in the SUV.

"Why are you putting that back in your car if you just brought it out?"

He slammed the door shut and turned to look at her. "Keep the animals away."

She glanced around, her brows drawing together. "What kind of animals?"

"Raccoons, deer—" he walked past her, leaning down to grab the two folding chairs he'd packed, "—elk, bears. The usual."

"Bears?"

He opened one of the chairs and set it down, glancing back at her.

"Yeah. Bears. They usually don't bug you if you're careful."

Her face had drained of all color. "Like, real bears?"

"No, like teddy bears, Allie." He gave a soft laugh. "Relax, you have nothing to worry about."

"Bears eat people."

"Not usually."

"This is wrong," she muttered, storming toward him. "Take me home. Please. Take me back to that shit motel. Anywhere but here."

He caught her wrists, holding her at distance. His gut twisted at the genuine fear he saw in her eyes.

"Hey, easy." He released one wrist and slipped an arm around her waist, pulling her close to hold her still. "Easy, there."

"I told you I'm not a camper." She glanced around. "I can't do this, Clint."

"You haven't even tried it yet." He brushed a strand of hair out her eyes and resisted the urge to lean down and kiss her again. "Give it a chance. I *know* you'll end up having fun, Allie. Nature is in your blood, you've just been ignoring it."

The fear in her gaze flickered out and was replaced with annoyance.

"Let me just remind you of something. This is *not* a vacation for me. I didn't choose to come with you. I should be back in Seattle talking some sense into Kenneth since you don't seem to have the balls to do it."

His jaw tightened. She just had to bring up Kenneth again. Why, every time he thought maybe he'd been wrong, did she have to remind him that she still might have feelings for Ken.

"Okay," he agreed mildly, "and it's not like you've just realized I'm keeping you away for the week. So why don't you just accept it already and try to enjoy yourself."

"Try to enjoy myself?" Her eyes widened and her lips went taut. "I don't think so, Clint. In fact, you know where I'm spending the majority of this trip?" She jammed her thumb toward the tent. "In there. With my book. So where is it?"

"Where's what?"

"The book you promised me."

"I didn't get you one." He kicked himself. Damn, he'd forgotten.

"But you promised."

"You fell asleep during the drive."

"Right. Blame me. Like any of this is my fault." She tugged away from him and stomped off toward the tent.

"Allie, wait."

She glared at him and tugged the flap up, then disappeared inside.

Clint sighed and shoved a hand through his hair. Hell, for a minute there it had looked as if their week together could be a less about fighting and more about the pleasure. And now she'd shoved him away again—physically and emotionally.

He adjusted his jeans, easing the pressure of denim against his cock. She wouldn't stay in there forever. Eventually Allie would have to come out.

Before this week was finished he was confident he and Allison would be lovers. He'd be killing two birds with one stone. When he finally returned her to Seattle, he would have scratched the *sleep with Allie* itch, and Kenneth would be safely married.

His mouth curved into a slight smile as he went to start the fire.

Allison sat on the sleeping bag on the inflatable bed, her legs drawn up to her chest and her chin on her knees.

She listened to the sound of some kind of frog-like thing coming from the lake behind them, and the crackling of the fire she could see burning outside the tent.

The reminder that she hadn't eaten in hours came from the angry growl in her stomach. She bit back a groan and breathed in the smell of cooking meat and smoke.

Clint had come in about an hour ago to invite her to sit by the fire while he cooked dinner. And she'd been damn tempted, because it was getting cold in this tent.

But she hadn't gone. Had stubbornly refused to respond and stayed put on the inflatable bed. Which, to her surprise, was rather comfortable.

How long had she been in this tent anyway? Sitting in the dark and cursing him out in her head. She'd given up trying to see anything. Once the sun had set, the only hint of light came from the fire outside.

Her stomach growled again.

"Dinner's done, Allie."

His carefree announcement from outside made her want to chuck something at him again. But it was a little hard being that he was out there and she was in here.

Folding her arms across her stomach she ground her teeth together and refused to answer. Who needed to eat? Food was overrated anyway.

Footsteps sounded outside the entrance to the tent, and she heard the pull of the zipper. A second later the silhouette of Clint hovered in the doorway.

"Maybe you didn't hear me."

"I heard you, I'm just not listening. There is a difference you know."

"Okay then." The flap fell down, shrouding the inside in darkness again.

Strong arms wrapped around her waist and hauled her off the bed.

"Clint, put me down!" She struggled against him as he hefted her higher into his arms.

"Can't do it. If by some chance you do try and file a police report later, the last thing I'm going to have added to it was that I starved you."

Anger bubbled up in her belly and she pounded her fists against his shoulders. "*I'm* choosing not to eat."

"Well, I'm choosing *for* you to eat." He pushed them out of the tent.

The brightness and smoke from the campfire stung her eyes. She blinked several times, her eyes watering.

"Have a seat." He deposited her into a folding chair.

Allison ground her teeth together and glared up at him. "You have this cave man mentality about you lately that can drive a girl nuts, you realize that?"

"Drive them nuts in a good way?"

"Not so much." Her lower lip jutted out and she turned to glare at the fire.

The heat slowly made its way through her body, easing the chill in her bones. She spotted hotdogs on sticks arched over the fire and her mouth watered. The fire spit and crackled, the wood shifting in the pit.

"Do you want a beer?"

She jerked her gaze back to his. "A beer?"

He sat in a folding chair just inches from hers and popped open a bottle. "There's water or beer. Take your pick."

She narrowed her eyes. God, she'd cut off her right arm for that beer after the last two days she'd had. But would it really be smart to mix alcohol and Clint?

"Come on, you know you want it." His grin widened and he leaned forward, waving the bottle in front of her face.

The hell with being smart. She snatched the bottle from his hand and leaned back in the chair again.

Bringing the bottle to her mouth, she took a long drink.

"Bun or no bun?"

She set the bottle down and looked at Clint again. He stared at her, a slight smile curving his lips. His profile flickered in the firelight.

"Bun." She didn't even pretend to not know what he referred to. She wanted that damn hot dog.

He pulled the stick from the ground and reached for the bag of buns nearby. After pulling the dog from the stick he laid it on the bread and handed it to her.

"Sorry, I didn't bring condiments."

She accepted the hot dog with a shrug. "I don't need any. Despite what you may think, I'm actually pretty low maintenance."

"Except when it comes to polyester."

"Hey, it irritates my skin." She waved the dog at him and scowled. "But I checked the label on this Pollyanna-style sweat suit you bought me, and it's mostly cotton. So I should be okay."

"Glad to hear it."

Allison sat the beer between her thighs and lifted the hot dog to her mouth. She took the first bite and nearly orgasmed on the spot.

"That good?"

She nodded. The hot dog tasted like no hot dog she'd ever eaten before. It was like the sovereign of all hot dogs.

"What brand is this?"

"I'm not really sure. Whatever was cheap."

She took another bite and gave him a suspicious glance. "Okay, I buy the cheap stuff, and it doesn't taste anything like this."

"Well, that's because you don't cook it over a campfire." He lifted his own beer and took a long swallow. "It makes them twenty times better. At least."

She watched the muscles of his throat work as he swallowed. Awareness and heat slid slowly through her body as she stared at him. Part of it was the beer kicking in, and part of it was just Clint.

When she'd told him he made her a little stupid, she hadn't been lying. The moment he touched her, or hell, even looked at her in that way, she became one big puddle. This was definitely new. Back in college he'd never affected her this way.

She lifted the beer and took a few hard draws.

"How about another beer since you're nearly done with that one."

She bit back a sigh. Why not? Already that one beer had improved her grumpiness a little.

"Sure." She finished the last bit in her current bottle and set it on the ground.

As Clint handed her another beer, she asked, "So the forest ranger thing. What gives? You never really said. I know you liked the outdoors as a kid, but what made you decide to go all the way? You get all hyper off those Smokey the Bear ads as a kid?"

"There's no 'the'."

She paused, the beer bottle halfway to her lips. "What?"

"It's Smokey Bear, not Smokey the Bear." He pointed his bottle toward her. "Everyone gets confused, because of this song written about him, and that's where the *the* came from."

She lifted an eyebrow and shook her head. "Wow, you learn something new every day. I didn't realize it was such a controversy."

"Ah, see, and it is." His mouth curved and he let out a soft laugh. "But Smokey's not the reason I decided to become a forest ranger."

"No?"

"Nah. Dad took me camping all the time." He glanced out over the lake. "Nature is in my blood. Being outside. Away from the chaos of the city."

She gave a slight nod. She could see that. The food was good, the fire was warm. It probably was pretty relaxing when you didn't have the stress of being kidnapped thrown in.

Her lips twitched as she finished off her hot dog, then chased it with another sip of beer.

When he'd come up during the summers, Clint had always challenged her to get outdoors more. Exploring the Arboretum, walking along any one of the beaches on the west side, or finding any places with trees to go nature walking.

Then the teen years had hit, and Kenneth had started to think about girls, and Allison's friends had started to *act* like girls and by the time Clint returned the next summer she'd become a little less outdoorsy and much more of the mall rat.

They'd still all hung out, but their activities tended to revolve around the movies and malls more. Maybe a beach walk every now and then. She felt a twinge of guilt. It totally hadn't been Clint's cup of tea, she could realize now, so why had he indulged her?

"Do you just hate the city or what?" she asked.

"I don't hate it." Clint leaned forward and kicked one of the logs on the edge of the fire. The wood shifted and the flames spit higher. "And I don't mind visiting. I just wouldn't want to live there."

"So do you live here?" She gestured to the woods around them. "Do you have some tiny cabin with the word Ranger above it?"

He laughed and reached for another beer. "No. This is where I come to relax. I live about an hour from here, closer to population."

"Shopping?" she asked with a smile.

"Depends on your idea of shopping."

"Hmm." She stretched her feet out, curling her toes in her shoes away from the fire.

He didn't say anything more, and she'd run out of things to say for the moment. She watched the way the firelight danced off the campsite as the steady crackling and shifting of wood calmed her.

Her body had warmed by now, from the fire and the alcohol. In fact she'd slipped comfortably into that peaceful state between relaxed and drowsy.

She tilted her head back in the chair and looked up at the stars through the break in the trees. Her brows drew together in fascination. So big and bright.

"They're pretty amazing, huh?"

"I haven't seen stars this bright since..." she trailed off. "Well, ever."

"Hmm. You remember that night," Clint began thoughtfully. "Back one summer when we snuck out of the house to go to a bonfire up in Richmond Beach?"

It didn't take long for the memory to come, and Allison's mouth twitched at the fond memory.

"Oh yeah. And we all went wading in Puget Sound with our jeans on? You kept threatening to throw me in all the way. That was a fun night..." She glanced up at the sky again. "I remember thinking the stars were huge, but they were nothing like this."

"No, they weren't. You were flirting that night with some guy. You two ever hook up?"

"Ah, yeah. Ricky. My first official boyfriend in high school. We weren't together long. He was a lousy kisser." *Nothing like you*, she almost added but bit her tongue before she could say the insane words.

Clint grunted. "Tomorrow night, if you want, we can hike to an area more open and get a better view of the entire night sky."

Her eyes drifted shut. "Tomorrow night?"

"Mmm hmm."

"How long are you really going to keep me here, Clint?"

When he didn't answer right away, she opened her eyes and turned to look at him again.

"I thought we discussed this, Allison. We'll come back Sunday night."

"Sunday night," she repeated, the disbelief surging up fast and strong again. When he'd first told her, she'd almost been convinced he was telling the truth. But over the past couple of days she'd realized he had to be just pulling a scare tactic.

And yet he kept saying it. One week. He would keep her for one week.

He had to be bluffing. She was ninety-eight percent positive. If he kept them up here until Sunday night, then he'd miss Kenneth's wedding. And there was no way Clint would miss that.

She'd wager he'd keep her here for two or three nights, tops. But surely not an entire week.

"All right." She shrugged and finished off the rest of her beer and grabbed another. "Whatever you say, buddy."

Chapter Nine

Clint stared at her, unease in his gut. She'd certainly seemed cavalier in her reply. Had almost seemed to brush him off. Maybe she didn't believe him.

He took a long draw on the beer. She probably thought he wouldn't want to miss Ken's wedding. She'd be wrong. He and Kenneth weren't that close anymore, and attending a black tie wedding made him a bit ill at ease just thinking about it.

If Allison thought he was bluffing about keeping her away for the week, it was probably better that way. It'd at least give him a few days of peace. Until the moment she realized he'd meant every word, then he'd have to start playing the dodging game again. The woman loved to throw things when she got upset.

He glanced up and watched as Allie downed half the beer in a few swallows. A few seconds later she stumbled to her feet. Jeez. Was she drunk? He'd forgotten what a lightweight she was.

"I need to wash my face."

His lips twitched, but he stifled the chuckle. He swung his arm and pointed to the lake.

"There's your faucet. If you want soap there's an environmentally friendly bottle of wash in that bag over there."

The air hissed out from her mouth, before she stomped off to grab the soap, before going down to the water's edge.

He set down his empty beer bottle and watched her.

The sweats tightened over her bottom when she bent down to the lake, and his gaze drifted over the curves of her body. Lord did he want her. Flat on her back. From behind. With her on top. On her hands and knees.

Hell, how long had it been since he'd had a woman? Months at least. His job and location made it harder to meet women. Of course the small town of Altwood was just under ten miles from his home, but most of the folks there were seniors, married with kids, or confirmed bachelors like himself. Not a whole lot of women in the part of Montana he lived.

"*Euggh.*" Allison rushed back from the lake and scowled. "If my face breaks out I am so not going to be happy."

"You look great," he said truthfully. Fresh faced with no makeup, skin glowing in the firelight.

"Hmm"

"Has anyone ever told you that you complain a lot?"

She cracked a smile. "I consider it bitching, and it's a skill I pride myself on."

He thought of the nightgown he'd bought her and his blood thickened. How would she react when he handed it to her?

"I'll be right back." She stood up again, knocking over a beer with her foot.

He watched as she fumbled her way into the tent. He could hear her moving about inside, muttering to herself.

A smile curved his lips and he stood to pick up the bottles. After cleaning up, emptying his bladder, and washing up in the lake, he finally made his way back to the tent.

His original plan had been to seduce Allie tonight, but something told him it might not be in the cards. He unzipped the tent and climbed inside, his glance falling on the bed.

Definitely not in the cards.

Allison lay sprawled out across the bed, still fully dressed but out cold.

"Well, you did give her beer," he muttered to himself and tugged off his T-shirt.

Once undressed, he walked over to her and tugged off her shoes. He managed to get her pants off without waking her, and decided to just leave her in the sexy-as-hell panties and shirt he'd bought her.

He tucked her into the sleeping bag and zipped it up to her chin. She barely stirred, just moaned as she snuggled around inside the cocoon.

He touched her cheek, grazing his finger over the soft skin. So sweet. God he'd really missed her over the years.

Clint settled into the sleeping bag next to her and sighed, hoping like hell he was wrong and she didn't really have any lingering feelings for Ken.

The next day Clint woke early. Naturally a morning person, it was instinct to leave the tent at the first crack of dawn to wash up quick in the lake and then go build a fire.

He'd slept hard last night. They both had. Allison was still asleep. She hadn't even stirred when he'd left the tent.

After crunching some newspaper in the fire pit, Clint laid some kindling on top. Crouching down, he lit a match and held it to the paper, watching it catch fire.

The zipper on the tent sounded and he jerked his head up, his blood pounding a little faster in the anticipation of seeing Allison.

It took a moment. He watched her small hands pry back the edges of fabric before her head popped out.

"Is it cold out there?" she asked groggily. Her hair was pulled back in a ponytail, but a few blonde wisps had escaped to fall around her hazel eyes.

"Probably."

She sighed and looked down at the ground, mumbling something.

"I'm sorry, I didn't quite catch that."

Her head snapped back up, her eyes flashing now. "I said I need to shower."

"There aren't showers here."

"Yes, I realize that." Her nose wrinkled. "But perhaps you could explain how one would bathe or shower while camping?"

"You bathe the same way you washed your face." He jerked his thumb toward the lake. "In there."

He heard the deep breath she drew in as her eyes drifted shut.

"That lake is pretty damn cold."

"Then don't bathe."

"Umm, gross. I need to shower and if freezing my ass off is the only way it'll happen, then I'll do it." She scowled and pulled her head back into the tent.

Clint bit back a laugh and walked over to the SUV, opening it and pulling out the bacon and eggs. This would probably be the only morning they could eat the good stuff. Once the ice melted in the chest, they'd be stuck with the dry foods unless he decided to make another run into town to grab some more ice.

Slamming the door shut again, he made his way back to the fire, food and a box of cooking supplies in his arms.

He'd just set down the supplies when Allison stepped out of the tent.

"I can't believe I'm camping," she grumbled. "Why couldn't you be a little more civilized and take me somewhere with plumbing? Maybe even a shower?"

"Not as much fun. Then I wouldn't get to see you naked as you bathe in a lake." He gave a roguish smile and opened the bacon, tearing off a strip and tossing it into the pan.

Her cheeks turned red. "You're not going to watch me."

"Sorry to break it to you," he gestured toward the lake. "But in case you didn't notice, there're no shower curtains around."

"Jackass," she muttered and grabbed a bottle out of the duffle bag, then hurried toward the lake. "Does your environmentally safe soap work on hair?"

"You can use it on any part of your body you want." He set the grate over the fire, then the pan on top of it.

"Don't look," she screamed and pulled off her clothes, striding naked into the water.

Good Lord in heaven. She was curvy temptation. The air rushed from between his clenched teeth and despite the fact he'd already bathed, he resisted the urge to strip naked and run in after her. Pick her up and wrap those long legs around his waist, then thrust straight into her hot center.

The smell of burning bacon snapped his attention from his growing hard-on. *Not now, buddy. You're cooking something else besides your hormones.*

"Shit, this water is freezing!"

He glanced up from the bacon and caught her rising from beneath the surface, water dripping down her body. His gaze locked on the drop that seemed suspended on the curve of her breast, before rolling down her nipple and falling back into the lake.

Disappointment set in when the erotic vision was blocked. She lifted the bottle of soap in front of her, squirting some into the palm of her hand. She lowered the bottle again and he bit back a groan.

She moved her hand over her body, leaving a sudsy film over her upper torso. Her gaze lifted to his and she arched a brow, slipping her hand beneath the water. A second later her lids fluttered shut and she bit her lip.

The little witch. She did that on purpose.

"Bacon's burning," she called throatily, a hint of a smile in her tone. "And I don't like mine burnt."

He cursed and dragged his focus back to the breakfast. Hell, she was right. The meat was almost black on one side. Grabbing a pair of tongs from the utensil box, he quickly flipped all the strips.

Another splash sounded and he glanced up to see her disappear under water. She reappeared a moment later and swam toward the shore.

She strode out and he had a moment to drool over her naked dripping body, before she wrapped a towel around her.

"That water is freezing," she said, teeth chattering.

"Get dressed. You'll be fine."

Her face, fresh and clean, scrunched together to display her displeasure.

"Will I? Because I'm pretty sure my nipples have turned to ice and are ready to break off." She rushed past him into the tent again.

An amused laughed bounced in his chest and he shook his head. Lord, some of the things Allie said just made him raise his eyebrows. She was so random. A little crazy at times. And, hell, definitely had moments when she was almost offensive. And yet...he'd always loved that about her. And he didn't really get offended by her swearing, no matter how many times he might chide her on the cursing habit.

He grabbed the tongs again and lifted the cooked bacon onto a plate, then went to crack a half-dozen eggs into the pan.

"Please don't burn those as well."

His lips twitched and he lifted his gaze to see her climbing out of the tent again. Attired in the pink sweat suit he'd bought and with her damp hair pulled back in a ponytail again, she was the image of squeaky-clean innocence.

Innocent? Yeah right. His gut twisted and his mouth went tight. That wasn't exactly a phrase he associated with Allie much.

Allison swallowed hard, keeping her chin high as she walked the distance from the tent to the campfire. Butterflies still ran rampant in her belly.

It had been damn hard to go run naked into that lake in front of him. But once she was in and had seen his gaze on her—the hot desire there, she'd responded. Had even found herself flirting like she was some professional exhibitionist. Damn it. What the hell did Clint do to her? The last thing she wanted was to encourage him into thinking they'd end up in bed together.

She'd been surprised to wake up this morning alone in her own sleeping bag. She'd been convinced he would try and seduce her again. Hell, it wasn't like he made it a secret those were his intentions.

And if she admitted it, she was a little disappointed he hadn't followed through. But could she really see it though? Sleeping with Clint? What happened after? And did she really want to risk damaging a friendship that had already been rocky for the past year?

Allison circled the fire and curled into the empty chair beside him. Through lowered lashes she took in his profile as he cooked their breakfast.

Hard jaw line, a nose that wasn't quite perfect because he'd broken it as a teen, but the flaw just made him that much sexier. Then there were those eyes, so blue and piercing. She slid her gaze down again to his lips, pursed with consternation as he moved the eggs around in the pan with a spatula.

Her cheeks warmed and she pressed a hand to her face, closing her eyes to the memory of his mouth moving over her body. He'd made her lose all control the other night. Had turned her into the most wanton, desperate, couldn't-think-of-anything-but-him-inside-her kind of woman.

"They're not burned."

Flustered, she opened her eyes again and met his gaze. "What?"

"The eggs."

"Oh. That's fine." She shook her head to clear the memories of last night. "I think I'm too hungry to care if they were."

Her stomach growled and she leaned back in the chair, crossing one leg over another.

"What's the plan today?"

"We're going canoeing."

"Nice. Are we going to sing campfire songs first at breakfast?" she drawled, glancing out at the lake. Her breath caught.

God, it really was amazingly beautiful with the sunlight sparkling on the blue water, casting diamond like shimmers over the lake.

He chuckled. "If you'd like. Hey, could you grab the coffee press out of the bag over there?"

With a sigh, and anticipating the warm beverage in her hands, she stood and walked over to the bag.

"How do you make coffee camping?"

"In the press. You boil water, which I've already done, put the grounds in the press and then pour the water on it." He gave her a sideways glance. "You ever use a coffee press?"

"Nope. I use a place called Ooo La Latté." She pulled out the press and walked it over to him.

"Thanks."

Their fingers brushed, and a spark of heat passed between them. He jerked his gaze to hers, his indrawn breath sharp. She watched his pupils dilate.

She took a quick step backward, her cheeks warming further. His free hand curled around hers, stalling her hasty retreat.

"Allison."

Her pulse jumped at how soft her name fell from his lips, the way he stroked his thumb over the palm of her hand. Her head spun and her knees turned rubbery.

"The eggs," she choked out desperately. "They're burning now."

He released her with a sigh and jerked the smoking eggs off the fire.

She folded her hands into tight fists and bit her lip.

"Sorry. Looks like most of the breakfast is burnt."

She feigned a casual shrug, even though her pulse still fluttered from his touch. "If it digests, we'll survive."

He dished her up a plate of food and gave her a considering glance. "Look at you. Toughening up after just one day."

"Toughening up?"

"Sure. I think the city chick might be getting broken in."

She snorted and accepted the plate he handed her, before sitting down. "You show me an outlet for my hair dryer and then we'll talk."

"You don't need it. It's drying just fine." He grinned and started making the coffee.

By the time he handed her a steaming mug full a few minutes later, she'd already scarfed down half her breakfast.

"You *were* hungry." He grinned and tucked himself back into the folding chair and stabbed at a chunk of eggs. "Camping does that to you. Makes even burnt food taste good."

She grunted and took another sip of coffee. The warm drink spread heat through her body and she gave a groan of approval.

"I love that."

"What?" She took another sip.

"That little sound you make when you're enjoying something," his voice roughened. "You make it a lot when I touch you."

"Can we not talk about that?" She lifted a burnt piece of bacon and chomped down on it. "It should never have happened between us, Clint. And please don't count on a repeat performance."

"Don't count on it?" His mouth curved upward. "Kitten, that's nothing compared to what you can expect tonight."

He was so damn confident they would become lovers. Too confident. Her heart skipped a beat.

Full now, she stood and dumped the few last bites of her eggs in the makeshift garbage bag.

Clint stood as well, though she noticed he'd managed to take out his entire plate of food in half the time.

She strode back toward the tent, but he caught her arm before she passed him, spinning her around.

The air rushed from her lungs as he pulled her body snug against his.

He cupped her chin in his calloused hands, firmly but without hurting her, and tilted her head up to meet his gaze. The heat and possessiveness there sent her heart fluttering in her chest.

Her knees threatened to buckle and she barely held back a weak groan.

"How about a morning kiss," he murmured softly, before dipping his head down and covering her mouth with his.

Lips, soft and firm, moved against hers, before his tongue traced the seam of her mouth. He tasted of coffee and man. Primitive and natural like the forest surrounding them.

This time she was unable to stop the soft groan, and his tongue slid past her lips to take advantage.

His palm against her back molded her body into his, as the delicious friction of his tongue against hers brought goose bumps to her flesh.

Though she knew this could only lead to something she wasn't emotionally prepared to explore, Allison couldn't push him away.

He angled her mouth to deepen the kiss. The palm of his hand slipped under her sweatshirt to move over her bare back.

Dampness gathered between her legs and a fierce throbbing built, until she gasped against his mouth and thrust her hips against his. Her head spun and the world around them faded. Her entire axis balanced on the man holding her. On Clint.

He lifted his mouth from hers, just barely and pressed his forehead against hers. His ragged breathing matched hers and she knew he was struggling with control as much as she.

Allison drew in an unsteady breath and didn't move, couldn't begin to think about tearing her body from the heat of his. Already her nipples had tightened almost painfully, and through the layers of clothing, brushed against his hard chest. She knew he felt it, how could he not?

He released her chin and moved both of his hands to bracket her waist. Clint traced his fingers over the bare flesh he'd exposed between the waistband of her sweats and her top before sliding up and dragging her sweater with it. He moved slowly over her ribcage and stopped just under the swell of her breasts.

He moved his thumbs against her flesh and she tensed, the air stranded in her chest. Her nipples ached, seemed to tighten further at the promise of his touch.

The word *please* hovered on her tongue. To beg for him to move the couple of inches upward, to have his fingers stroking and toying with the sensitive tips.

His fingers remained where they were, swirling circles against her flesh. His warm breath feathered across her mouth, mingling with hers.

It was almost like they were at a stand-off. To see who would break first. Would she do it? Beg him to touch her or let loose the ragged groan that she barely withheld? Or would he finally just do it—touch her like she wanted him to?

His lips brushed just barely across hers again and another rush of moisture gathered inside her.

"Please." The word left her lips as half gasp, half groan.

His growl was a masculine sound of pure triumph, echoing in her head, just before he slid his fingers up her breasts to capture the tips through her bra.

He covered her mouth hard with his, pinching her nipples between rough fingers and squeezing. His touch was far from gentle, and damn it, exactly how she loved it. He knew her. Somehow he knew exactly what she wanted.

He sucked her tongue into his mouth, grazing his teeth across it before soothing it with his own.

Spirals of pleasure moved up through her body, dizzying her and robbing her of all ability for coherent thoughts. He pushed down the cups of her bra and his hands cupped her naked breasts. His mouth tore from hers and he looked down at her.

"Those nipples," he muttered thickly. "Damn. So pink and pretty."

Her nipples scraped against the roughened texture of his palms and she whimpered, her knees definitely turning to liquid this time.

Clint's head lowered, the stubble on his chin grazed her flesh, before closing his mouth around one aching tip. Her eyes drifted shut as pleasure seared through every inch of her. She gripped his shoulders, not trusting herself to remain upright as he suckled her.

Wanting to see his head against her breast, Allison opened her eyes again. And shrieked.

Clint snapped his head up in shock as she shoved away from him. She stumbled half-naked, still screaming, to one of the camp chairs and climbed onto it.

Laughing now, Clint tried to shoo away the raccoon rummaging through their bag of garbage.

"You can come down, Allie," he said a moment later, grabbing the garbage. "I'll put this in the car. Can't believe that little guy was so bold."

"Little? That thing could've eaten a cat," she grumbled, pulling the lace cups of her bra back over her breasts and tugging her shirt back down.

After Clint returned he looked at her and sighed, the disappointment on his face evident as he noted she'd adjusted her clothes on again.

He glanced toward the water. "Well, since the raccoon killed the mood, we may as save the rest of the fun for tonight and get ready to canoe."

Chapter Ten

Allison stared at Clint, watched that veil of control slip back over his persona. He was always able to turn it on and off like a switch. And he actually thought she'd just immediately agree to have sex when he snapped his fingers and declared it the right time.

Irritated with him and herself, she ground her teeth together and climbed off the chair.

"Why don't you grab the windbreaker out of the duffle bag in the tent?" His voice seemed altogether too calm as he moved away from her completely. "I'll soak our dishes and then get the canoe set to go. We'll head out in a few."

Her body still humming from his touch and her mind screaming with frustration, she moved past him toward the tent.

She found the blue windbreaker in the duffle bag and tugged it on over her sweat outfit. Good Lord. Sweats. When was the last time she'd worn them? When was the last time she'd worn pants period?

The image of the Betsey Johnson blue teardrop dress hanging in her closet flickered through her head. With a wistful sigh, she tugged up the zipper of the ugly jacket and pushed it down on her hips. God, the thing was huge and anti-feminine.

She unzipped the tent again and climbed out without any difficulty. Clint was right about one thing, she was starting to get the hang of this camping thing.

And the air. He'd been right about how amazing it was. She closed her eyes and drew in another breath. The smell of trees—what were they? Pine?—and the crisp clean smell of the lake filled her senses.

"Ready?"

She glanced up to where he stood near the water's edge. Damn, he looked good. So *nature boy*. Framed in front of the glistening lake, he was all man. The blue shirt he wore stretched taut across his broad chest and his calves were all muscle beneath the long khaki shorts.

She turned her focus to the canoe behind him. Her pulse skipped and she blinked with dismay. She could not be excited about going out on the lake, could she?

"Allie?"

"Ready." She gave a brisk nod and started toward the lake.

"Hang on," he held up his hand to stop her. "Can you run back to the car and grab my camera? The wind's not too bad today and I'd love to take some shots with the lake still."

Without answering, she turned and headed back to his car.

She grabbed the camera on the front seat and was about to shut the door when she spotted his cell phone. Not the keys to his car, but definitely a key to getting help if she decided she wanted it.

Allison flipped it open, ready to dial. Her heart sank at the three little words staring back at her. *No service available.*

She slipped the cell phone into the pocket of her windbreaker, reassured just having it on her.

"Got it." She slammed the door and hurried back to the lake.

"Great, thanks." He took the camera from her and their fingers brushed again.

More tingles raced through her body, but she tried harder to ignore them.

"Here, let me help you into the canoe." He took her hand and assisted her as she stepped into the boat. "You ever been in one of these before?"

"Can't say that I have." She walked to the end and sat on the wooden seat, facing out toward the lake. "Is there no motor?"

"No motor crafts allowed on this lake." He climbed in and set the boat rocking.

Her chest tightened and she gripped the wooden edge of the boat. "Are you sure this thing is safe?"

His laugh reverberated in the vast openness around them. "People have been using these babies for centuries, Allie. They're perfectly safe."

"Hmmmph." She didn't bother to hide her skepticism.

"And not only that, you're also going to help steer."

She blinked and turned around, her gaze dropping to the long paddle he held out her. "Steer?"

"Yes. Teamwork, Allie."

"You're determined to turn me into a happy camper, aren't you?" she grumbled, but took the paddle from him. "It ain't going to happen."

"It already is happening." His lips twitched as he turned and pushed the paddle into the water, pushing them away from the water's edge.

The moment the boat lost purchase on the bottom of the lake, it began to rock a little more.

"Clint." Her voice rose as panic assailed her.

"We're fine. Just hang on to your paddle until I tell you to put it into the water."

He moved to the middle seat and sat down, facing her back.

"I'm going to turn us to the east then I'll have you start to paddle as well."

She didn't answer, just turned away from him again and glanced out over the edge of the lake. The surface barely moved, just had tiny ripples from where his paddle dipped into the dark blue depths.

"Okay. Go ahead and put your paddle into the water on the right side."

Taking a deep breath she slid the paddle off the edge of the canoe into the water.

"Just like that. Good. Now push through, then lift it out and repeat," his voice encouraged. "Good job. You're doing great, Allie."

His praise shouldn't have pleased her, but it did. Ridiculously so. She flushed and continued making the jerky strokes, until she finally found a rhythm that worked for her.

The canoe glided through the water, taking them further out onto the lake. Comfortable with paddling now, she glanced up and took a moment to really drink in the view.

The sight was literally breathtaking, stealing away her ability to draw in a full breath and tightening her chest. Everything around her was bigger than life. The dark crystal blue of the lake and massive peaks of the mountains in the distance. So rugged, raw and seeming untouched.

A view that must've been relatively unchanged for centuries.

"You've stopped paddling."

She flushed and pressed her paddle back into the water again.

"It takes your breath away, doesn't it?" he asked, his voice tinged with awe.

"Yes." She didn't deny it and drew in another lungful of the crisp clean air. "It's amazing."

"I love to come out here and camp every now and then."

"Wait, you don't actually work up here?"

"No. I like isolation every once in awhile, but all the time? Nah, can't handle it."

"So you work around people?"

When she'd first learned Clint had become a forest ranger, she'd basically assumed he lived way off in the woods and spent his days talking to Bambi.

"Yes. I work around people. In fact probably my favorite part of the job is when I give guided tours to the kids."

Her eyebrows shot up. "For real?"

"Yeah. Schools bring kids in for field trips all the time. Kids are fun. So curious and honest. The honesty part cracks me up sometimes." He gave a soft laugh and she couldn't help but notice how his voice had changed when he'd mentioned the kids.

This was a man who wanted to be a father. She knew it without a doubt. But then, Clint had always been patient with kids. Her stomach warmed and she swallowed against the sudden tightness in her throat.

"Though the bulk of my work is spent isolated, I work with people at times," he went on, as if sensing they'd gone into deeper waters with their topic. "And though my house is pretty close to the park, the town is just about a ten-minute drive away."

Relieved at the change of subject, her ears perked up at the new topic. "Is there a place that does manicures?"

"Manicures?"

"Nails. A place that does nails." She glanced down at her fingers as she pulled the paddle out of the water. "By the time you come to your senses and return me to civilization, I'm going to need one hell of a job."

Clint's laugh sent a warm shiver down her spine.

"I don't know. There may be one around, I've never checked."

"No mall?"

"Nope. Couple of mom and pop shops."

"Wow." She tilted her head and nodded. "Small town."

"Definitely won't find a McDonalds."

"That could be argued to be a good thing."

The canoe slowed and she glanced over her shoulder to figure out why he'd stopped paddling.

He stared back at her, his blue gaze had narrowed somberly. "Is it really that bad? Being out here?"

Her breath caught again and she turned around to look out off the front of the canoe.

Once again the view around them rocked her to her core. Made her feel small and insignificant. Made her feel kind of stupid for bringing up getting a manicure. Her stomach clenched and she swallowed hard. Maybe she had become a little superficial...

"No," she said softly. "It's not bad at all. It's pretty damn amazing actually."

The water around them stirred as he dipped the paddle into the lake again, then the canoe surged forward.

"Hang on," he called out as she began to lower her paddle back into the water. "Let me turn us toward the shore over there. I want to show you something."

She relaxed and waited until he gave her the okay to paddle again, before dipping back into the water. They steered closer to the shoreline before the canoe slowed again. She glanced behind her to see Clint holding his paddle still in the water to bring them to a stop.

He leaned forward and his warm breath feathered across the curve of her ear. Tingles raced down her spine as warmth eased through her body.

"Okay, now look at the shore," he said quietly. "Toward that really dense group of trees."

She had to refocus her gaze, since it had started to cross from each warm word he spoke against her ear.

"What am I looking for?"

"Talk quietly," he commanded, his voice still barely audible.

Talk quietly. Good Lord. What was the guy afraid of? Scaring the fish? She searched the shore and started to shake her head. Hissing, "I don't see—*oooh*."

Her eyes widened and tension rocked through her muscles. The bear she'd just spotted stepped out from one of the trees and glanced at them, before wandering along the shoreline.

"Oh God. It's a bear," she whispered. "For real. That's a bear."

"Yes, for real that's a bear." He paddled them closer. "Do you have my camera?"

She laid the paddle across the canoe and fumbled in her pocket for his camera. Turning around, she handed him the small device and then spun back to watch the bear.

It wandered along the shoreline, in and out of trees, paying little attention to them. A shiver ran down her spine, but this time it was from fear.

They weren't that far from the campsite. They'd only paddled for about five minutes. And there were bears this close?

"Does that kind of bear eat humans?"

Clint laughed again, then she heard the click of the camera go off as he took a picture.

"The black bear is more likely to eat your food than you, Allie."

"I don't know," she muttered. "Let's just say I'm glad we're on a lake right now."

The camera clicked again. "Doesn't really matter. Bears can swim."

"*What?*" Her voice carried across the water and the bear glanced out their way.

"It's true. A bear can easily swim across a lake."

"Where's my fucking paddle?" She fumbled to get the paddle in the water again. "We are so out of here."

"Easy." Clint's sudden hand on her shoulder gave a reassuring squeeze.

"Bears freak me out."

"They freak a lot of people out." His other hand descended upon her shoulder and he started to massage the fear out of her. "I promise you, humans generally aren't on their diet."

"Hmm." She narrowed her eyes, and eyed the bear warily. *Come after me, buddy, and you'll get a paddle shoved so far up your—*

136

"Besides, you have to admit she's beautiful."

She grunted. "She is. Scary, but beautiful."

They fell into silence, watching the bear wander around. Another movement caught her eye. Her mouth parted on a gasp as a smaller bear bounded out from the trees.

"Her cub." His warm breath tickled her ear.

"It's so cute! Take a picture of it." When he didn't immediately move to comply, she moved her arm behind her to elbow him in the ribs. "*Hurry.*"

He gave a soft chuckle before his hands slid from her shoulders to grab the camera again.

The disappearance of the warmth of his touch sent a small ache of loss through her, but she ignored it as she focused on the sight in front of her.

She watched the mother bear and cub wander along the lake's edge, in and out of trees scavenging for food. It was like something on the freaking nature channel. Never could she imagine that she'd be up this close—seeing it for herself. It was amazing, so touching, her eyes pricked with tears.

"All right. Grab your paddle, we'll head further out down the lake."

After one last lingering glance at the bears, she grabbed her paddle again and waited for Clint to guide her.

They stayed on the lake for another hour at least, observing more wildlife. Deer, elk and eagles. Her mind overflowed with images and sensations.

"I don't suppose you'd be up for a small hike?" Clint asked.

"Actually, yeah. I think it could be fun. Great substitute for my usual step class," she teased, surprised she was actually excited about exploring the area.

Clint pulled the canoe ashore and led her on a hike that lasted another couple of hours. When she'd complained of hunger, Clint was ready with yet another granola bar. This time she didn't quite mind the nuts and berries, they held her over longer than any sugary bar would have.

By the time they arrived back at the campsite the sun was beginning to set and Clint must have taken close to a hundred pictures.

"You wore me out," she murmured after helping him drag the canoe to shore.

Though her muscles ached, her body seemed to be on high alert for his touch. During their day he'd often get a little too close—whisper something in her ear. Or grab her hand to help her keep her balance on the hike. And of course each touch had brought her right back to the warm fuzzies status.

Allison tried to shove away the reminder as she stumbled over to the folding canvas chair near the campfire and collapsed into it, rubbing her aching calves.

Keep it friends, Allison, friends is so much simpler.

"You did great today," Clint said, glancing down at Allie and giving a slight smile.

She *had* done great. The realization pleased him. Confirmed what he already knew, that Allison was more than just a pretty face. That the fun, carefree girl he'd once known was still hiding inside, she just needed a little coaxing to come out.

"Are you hungry for dinner?" he asked.

"God, yes. But, please, no more granola bars."

"No granola bars." His lips twisted. She probably wouldn't care much for the other options though. "I was thinking more along the lines of whole wheat pitas stuffed with tuna, and dried fruit on the side."

"Hmm. I don't suppose I could convince you to whip up some chicken Parmesan?"

His loud laugh cracked through the trees. "Sorry, kitten. The bacon was the last of the meat we had. The ice in the cooler only lasts so long." He paused. "Or I could break out the freeze-dried chicken and potatoes. But I was going to save that for tomorrow night."

Her eyes snapped open and her brows drew together. "Umm...eew. Tuna please."

"Don't knock it until you try it. It's actually pretty good," he said, before heading to the SUV to grab the food out of the back.

When he returned he handed her the food. "Since I made breakfast, I thought you could help out and make dinner." He winked. "I'm going to build the fire."

Allison wrinkled her nose but didn't protest. He smiled at the small victory, then went to set up the kindling and paper for the fire.

"Is there a can opener?"

"In the bag over there."

He struck a match and held the flame to the kindling and paper. A few minutes later the fire was crackling and licking heat into their campsite.

"Here you are."

He glanced up and found Allie holding out the tin plate with his dinner on it. He rose to his feet and accepted the food.

"Not bad, Allie, not bad. We'll make a camper of you yet," he teased, expecting her to protest or make some scalding remark.

She surprised him, though, when her face flushed and pleasure shimmered in her eyes.

"Thanks," she finally said and moved to sit down in her chair, clutching her own plate as she picked at her food.

Interesting.

Clint lifted the pita and took a bite. The tuna hit the spot, easing his hunger for protein, and he polished it off within minutes before moving on to the dried fruit.

By the time he'd finished his dinner, she'd eaten nearly half of hers.

He stood and took his plate over to the hand pump, a few yards away, rinsing it off. Soft footsteps behind him notified him of Allison's presence.

"You done already?" he asked, noticing his voice sounded scratchier than usual.

Damn. There'd been a tickle in the back of his throat since last night. He brushed off the possibility he was getting sick. He never got sick. Hell the last time had been...a couple of years at least.

"Yeah," she answered as she took her turn washing off her plate. "I'm going to bathe in the lake and go to bed."

"You already bathed this morning."

"Yeah but we spent all day getting sweaty under the hot sun," she pointed out with a teasing scowl, then headed back toward the lake.

He noted with surprise that she wasted no time. Just stripped off her clothes and dove into the water before he even had a chance to appreciate her nakedness.

His body stirred to life and he clenched his jaw, willing his dick to settle down.

She emerged a few minutes later, apparently happy with the quick rinse. After grabbing her clothes, she hurried past him, breasts and ass jiggling as she made her way into the tent. Maybe she was getting a little *too* comfortable with this nature stuff.

His body was definitely reacting now. Christ, she'd be lucky if he didn't have her flat on her back before the moon had fully risen. What the hell. Did she *want* him to lose control? Who ran around bare-assed naked in front of the opposite sex and didn't expect a response?

"Hey, Clint?" Her sweet voice rang out from inside the tent. "I thought you said you bought me some pajamas. Where are they?"

He opened his mouth then shut it again. Hmm. Maybe that impulse buy on the pajamas hadn't been the best choice. She certainly wouldn't find a flannel nightgown in the bag.

"Clint?"

"I did," he said calmly. "They're in the plastic bag inside the duffle bag."

He listened to her unzip the bag and search through it, then the rustle of the bag.

"Oh my God."

Trying to figure out if that had been a good *Oh my God*, or a bad one, Clint stood again and began to clean up the rest of their dinner.

He heard her step out of the tent again, and he glanced over, not sure what he'd find.

She had another pair of sweats on, and gripped the silky nightgown in her fist. It took him a half a second to realize she was making a beeline toward the fire with it.

"Oh no you don't." He dropped the trash and caught her wrist before she could toss it into the flames.

Allison tugged at her hand. "I am not wearing this."

"Fine. Sleep naked then."

Her lips parted, and the green in her hazel eyes more prominent in the firelight.

"You're not funny, Clint."

He plucked the nightgown from her fingers and put it safely behind his back.

"I'm not trying to be funny."

Her cheeks reddened. "You buy me a sweat suit my grandmother would wear, and a nightgown that would make her blush."

His mouth curled. "It's actually quite decent. It covers all the pink areas, and—"

"I am *not* wearing it."

"Great. I'd much prefer you naked anyway."

"*Oh.*" Her fists clenched at her side and she swallowed hard "I'm not sleeping with you. If that was your motive in buying it."

"Allie, why are you fighting the inevitable?" He stepped closer and caught her chin between his fingers. Determination rushed through his blood. And desire, hot and potent. "You want me, and I want you, kitten. More than you know. Last night I let you sleep without sharing my sleeping bag. That's not going to happen again tonight."

Her eyes widened and he heard the shift in her breathing as a visible tremble ran through her body.

"I'll just wear the sweats to bed," she said with husky defiance.

"I'll take them off."

Her face flushed and her lower lip trembled. "I shouldn't be surprised, Clint. Not after you tied me to the bed the other night."

"I did." He paused and lowered his head closer to hers. "And you know what, Allison? You liked it."

Her breasts rose sharply, the tips just brushing in a light contact across his chest. He barely stopped the strangled groan that threatened, even as his cock hardened.

"Did not," she whispered, her eyelids fluttering closed.

"Did too." He pushed the nightgown back into her hands and then brushed his mouth against hers. "Now go change. I'll join you in a few minutes."

She shook her head and pulled away. "Why are you determined to make this happen? It's going to destroy our friendship."

Because she'd been a fever in his blood since she'd stopped looking like a gangly teen, and had developed the luscious curves of a woman. Because he'd been out of his mind with jealousy when Kenneth had made the moves on her. Because if he didn't have her soon he was going to explode.

"Why are you determined for it not to happen?" His gut twisted as he waited for the response he didn't want to hear. That she still had feelings for Kenneth.

She watched him for a moment, then instead of answering, turned and went into the tent, zipping it shut behind her.

Damn. Clint thrust a hand through his hair and shook his head. His dick had been half hard all day from wanting her so badly. Every time he touched her she just about begged him to take her, so why—when he laid it out on the table—did she still fight it? Fight what was between them?

He kicked dirt onto the fire and it hissed in response, dying out in certain spots. Grabbing the bucket he went to the lake to fill it up so he could put out the rest of the fire.

Hell, if it was only as easy to douse his desire for Allie.

Chapter Eleven

Allison blinked rapidly inside the tent to adjust her vision. Her heart hadn't stopped pounding since Clint had calmly stated that he intended to have her tonight. As if she had no say in the matter.

But do you really want to say no? She smothered the taunting voice in her head and let out a growl of frustration.

Sleeping with Clint was a bad idea. Wasn't it? Dating Kenneth had definitely diluted her friendship with him a bit, did she really want to make the same mistake with Clint? Even if their friendship had seemed to go downhill in the past year anyway.

She tossed the nightgown on the inflatable bed, then pulled off her sweatshirt and shoved down her pants. Once again naked, she grabbed the nightgown and tugged it on.

She'd been so close to saying to hell with it and sleeping in the sweats. But the steely determination she'd seen in Clint's gaze had convinced her he'd probably strip her himself—and enjoy doing it. Her body heated at the thought and she groaned.

The silky nightgown fell across her body is a soft whisper. It wasn't unpleasant, but it certainly did little to ward off the cold. Her nipples peaked beneath the silk and gooseflesh broke out on her arms.

Biting her lip, she hurried to the bed and unzipped her sleeping bag. She climbed inside, her body tense with expectation. Would he come in and demand she get in his bag? Be a total Neanderthal about his promise to have her? The hell with that. She'd bite his lip off.

The rasp of the zipper announced Clint's entrance to the tent. Her body went rigid and she held her breath. The faint light from some kind of lamp he held cast shadows inside the tent.

Would he come over?

She heard another zipper rasp and heat rushed through her body. Images of him taking off his jeans flooded her head. The rustle of his clothes hitting the floor brought moisture between her legs.

"Did you change?"

His gruff question sent her irritation meter up another notch. She ground her teeth together, not willing to answer. Excited to see what would happen if she didn't.

Footsteps sounded, coming closer to her side of the bed. He set the lamp next to the bed and knelt down. When he reached for the zipper on the sleeping bag she slapped his hand away.

"Yes," she said quickly. "I changed."

He caught her wrist and pushed it back to the mattress above her head.

"Now you don't mind if I check for myself, do you, kitten?"

"Actually, I do," she said, clinging to that last bit of defiance, even as her heart slammed against her ribcage with excitement. It was so wrong that this was turning her on. Wasn't it?

Don't sleep with him, Allison, you'll regret it in the morning.

"Do you really?" He caught her other wrist and lifted it up beside the first, then adjusted his grip to pin both her wrists above her head in one of his hands.

He reached for the zipper again and this time she couldn't protest, her tongue was thick in her mouth. The ache between her legs intensified and her breasts swelled.

The cool air brushed her near naked skin, followed by his sharp indrawn breath.

"You wore it."

Her heart thundered in her chest, it grew difficult to breathe. "You're surprised? You didn't really give me a choice."

"No, I didn't," he agreed and reached out to trace the neckline of the nightgown, which was cut low on her breasts.

Her nipples pebbled and she bit back a groan, turning her head so he couldn't see the desire she fought. A girl had to have some pride.

"You've seen I'm wearing it. Now let me go," she said huskily.

Their gazes connected and the possessive heat is his eyes sent another rush of moisture between her legs.

"I'm not sure I can do that." Still watching her, he slid his hand downward to cup her breast. "And I'm pretty sure you don't really want me to."

The breath locked in her throat and her nipple tightened against his palm. His fingers slid inward to capture the tip and she couldn't stop the choked gasp that escaped.

"Clint," she whispered.

"What?" His thumb moved lightly back and forth over her nipple. "You want me to stop doing this?"

Tingles spread from the point where he stroked, up to her fingers still held above her head.

"Or this?" His head lowered and his mouth replaced his fingers, capturing the tip between soft lips.

Her back arched as pleasure spread to every inch of her body.

The flat of his tongue laved the tip through the silk of the nightgown. The longer he did it, the damper the fabric became and the more intense the sensation. Her breath came out in jerky little puffs.

"Or maybe this." With a growl he drew the entire nipple into his mouth and sucked hard.

Each pull he made on her breast sent a sharp ache straight down between her legs.

She squirmed beneath him, pulling at her wrists but he made no move to release her.

His free hand slid over her belly, scrunching the silky nightgown as he continued to suck on her nipple.

The fingers fanned downward to her lower abdomen. The pressure of his hand on her body only heightened the intensity of the pleasure.

So close. If he'd just moved his hand a little lower. God she needed those fingers teasing her. Inside her. Her hips lifted against his hand and she twisted in his hold.

He lifted his mouth from her, barely a hair and muttered, "Or maybe you want me to stop doing this."

The hand on her stomach moved lower. Slowly. Entirely too slowly. His fingertips brushed the swell of her mound through her panties and she froze, the breath stranded in her lungs.

He slid his fingers just a little further until they nestled against her cleft.

"So warm." He pressed a kiss to her stomach and she heard the deep breath he drew in. "God, you smell good." His fingers tapped lightly against her mound and her mind spun. "You tasted good, too, the other night."

"Oh God." She groaned and let her legs fall open wider.

He lifted his head from her stomach and looked at her. "You're so wet. So incredibly hot for me."

She shook her head from side to side, all ability to talk completely gone.

His warm breath feathered against her stomach. "Tell me no, Allie. Tell me no and I swear to you I'll get up and go to sleep."

"No...I don't want you to stop." She squeezed her eyes shut. "Please don't stop."

Clint groaned and tugged her panties to the side. The fingers he thrust inside her weren't gentle, but her body was ready for him. Welcomed the ruthless invasion.

"Jesus," he whispered raggedly, his eyes shutting. "You feel good."

He went silent. His fingers taking over the conversation as they moved slowly inside her, taking her.

Every muscle in her body went lax, she made no effort to free her wrists anymore, instead reveled in the strength of the callused hand that held her. Focused only on the pleasure of having his fingers inside her.

Clint exhaled heavily, his warm breath tickling her stomach, before he jerked the nightgown up around her waist.

He sat up slightly as he stared down at her.

With the faint light from the lamp, his face remained half in shadow. But it was enough to see the raw desire there. She lowered her gaze to the unmistakable bulge in his boxers.

She swallowed hard and she squeezed her muscles around his fingers inside her, already imagining his erection replacing them.

When she lifted her gaze from his groin, she found him watching her.

The hand holding her wrists released one of her hands. Curling his fingers around the other, he dragged it down his body and pressed it against his swollen flesh.

Drawing in a swift breath, she held his challenging gaze and wrapped her fingers around his thickness through the boxers.

Heat flickered in his gaze, his nostrils flared.

She licked her lips, testing his length and width with the tips of her fingers.

"Feel something you like, kitten?"

"I might."

He growled low in his throat and pulled his fingers from her body and sat up. He pushed down his boxers, kicking them off the bed. His erection sprang free, brushing against her hand. She reached for it again, curling her fingers around his silken steel flesh.

"You might, huh?"

She bit back a groan. "Okay, I do."

"That's more like it." He reached down and grasped her nightgown, tugging the straps off her shoulders and pulling it down her body.

Exposed to the cool air in the tent, her breasts tingled and the tips grew tighter.

"Hurry," she begged as a shiver racked her body.

"You've got goose bumps." He traced a finger over the curve of one breast.

150

"That's because I'm cold." Which was only partially true.

"I'll warm you." His finger moved to the hardened tip of her breast and almost painful tingles rocked through her body.

He leaned down with a low growl and sucked one nipple into his mouth. Drawing hard on it, before grazing his teeth across the sensitive flesh and releasing it with a pop.

"I could suck on these all day."

Heat spread through her body and she bit her lip, closing her eyes. Clint's dirty talk again surprised her, though it shouldn't have after last night. And it aroused her. Made her hotter. Wetter.

His hand slid down to cup the swell of her sex again.

"But this," his voice lowered. "I want it again. I want you riding my tongue. Your taste in my mouth."

Her mind spun with the erotic visions his words created, and she couldn't have responded if she'd wanted to.

He moved down her body again, his mouth at the top of her panties.

"Do you want my mouth on you, Allison?"

His warm breath just above her clit made her gasp and lift her hips.

"Yes," she whispered.

"Say it."

"I want your mouth on me."

"Where do you want my mouth?"

Her cheeks burned hotter, embarrassment scorching a path through her blood.

He nuzzled her through the thin panties. "Tell me, kitten. I want to hear you say it."

"Clint." She lifted her hips, urging his head down. "Oh God, please."

"Say it, Allison. Say that dirty word that's on the tip of your tongue."

She closed her eyes. "I want your mouth on my pussy."

His knowing laugh was entirely too arrogant, but she didn't give a damn the moment his mouth closed over her. Even with the thin panties as a barrier it was all moisture, pressure and heat.

He thrust his tongue into her slit, pressing the panties deep inside her. His murmur of approval just impaled her onto that spiral of pleasure.

Her hips arched on the mattress, her hands fisting in the sleeping bag.

"*Please.*"

He gripped the fabric of her thong and ripped. The sound of fabric tearing overpowered their heavy breathing.

"I bought you at least twelve pairs," was his only apology for destroying her panties.

His hands slid under her bottom and lifted her back to his mouth. She whimpered at the slick invasion of his tongue inside her channel and ground herself against his face, opening her legs wider.

He lifted his head a bit. "Like that, do you? How about this?"

His mouth closed over her swollen nub at the same moment he pushed two fingers back inside her.

She only lasted a few seconds before the spiral of pleasure peaked, spilling over into an orgasm. Her hips lifted and her thighs clenched, unintelligible words fell from her lips.

"That didn't take long," he murmured, sliding back up her body.

"Mmm." She pressed a hand over her eyes, her heart still thundering in her chest and her body still trembling.

"We're not done." His mouth closed over the fast beating pulse in her neck.

"I don't want to be done." She drew one hand down the muscles of his chest while his tongue flicked over her skin.

Even though she'd just climaxed, heat still stirred low in her body.

She heard a rustle and opened her eyes to find Clint putting on a condom. He was such a boy scout. Always prepared.

He moved over her, the weight of his body pressing her down into the mattress. He used his knees to push her legs open again, then his thick erection prodded at her entrance.

He met her gaze and the heavy desire in his eyes was blatant.

"I can't be slow tonight," he said roughly. "I've wanted you for too long, Allie."

Pleasure spread through her, but not from his touch this time. From his words. He'd wanted her. For how long? Before this week?

She drew in a slow breath and looked at him from beneath her lashes. "Anyway you want me, Clint, you can have me."

His nostrils flared and he braced one hand on the mattress, using the other to line up his cock. He slid just barely past her folds, then with a groan thrust deep.

Her mouth parted on a gasp and she threw her head back, digging her nails into his shoulder. The way he filled her. Oh damn. So perfect. His width stretched her, pressed deeper.

"Jesus," he breathed. "I knew you'd feel good, but this..."

She attempted to lock her feet on the mattress, but her legs slipped on the bottom of the sleeping bag.

Clint's body followed where hers went. When she finally found purchase with her feet, he thrust back deep into her body when her hips lifted.

"You're a damn wet dream," he muttered and the hand on her hip slid inward. "You've always been my personal wet dream."

His words sent a shocking amount of pleasure through her that coincided with his thumb wiggling between her folds to find the sensitive nub.

"You're going to come for me again, kitten." He increased the pressure and a flush of pleasure moved up her body, tightening her nipples.

"Oh yeah?" she challenged on a gasp. "Make me."

"Easily."

His thumb, damp from her juices, circled her nub. The muscles in her bottom clenched as another wave of pleasure spiraled through her.

"All—" he pulled out of her a bit, "—too—" then slammed back inside her, "—easy."

He pinched her swollen clit between two fingers, spiking her into another orgasm. Her body trembled and waves of white flashed behind her closed lids. Her inner muscles clamped around his dick, drawing a ragged gasp from him.

She dragged her nails down his chest as waves of pleasure continued to rock her.

He made one last thrust deep into her, not quite as steady. His drawn-out groan filled the tent, demonstrating his own lack of control.

He stopped bracing himself above her and the weight of his body fell heavily on top of her, sinking her deeper into the blown-up mattress. His face burrowed into the curve of her neck.

She could feel the heavy pounding of his heart beneath the slick skin of his chest. The rapid flutter matched hers.

She made no effort to speak or push him off her, just moved her hands up and down his damp back. It had been perfect. Amazing and natural. *Emotional.* Like they'd been waiting years for this to happen. Oh God, was she falling for him? For *Clint*? Or was this just about the sex? She knew the answer before that second thought settled.

Uneasy with the intensity of her realization, she tightened her arms around him and took a moment to enjoy the sensation of him still imbedded deep inside her.

She brushed a tender kiss over his shoulder. "That was incredible."

"Mmm. Not thinking about breaking up a wedding now, are you, kitten?" he teased.

She stiffened beneath him, her fingers pausing in their idle tracing of his skin.

"Shit," Clint muttered. "I don't know why I said that, Allie."

But it was too late. All her tender emotions vanished as humiliation and anger rushed through her. Had he slept with her to take her mind off Kenneth? Had fucking her been a *distraction*?

She closed her eyes, a bitter taste in her mouth. Wanting to hurt him as much as he'd hurt her, she said tightly, "Just because you were the man inside my body, Clint, doesn't mean you were the one inside my head."

Clint's sudden stillness sent a wave of apprehension through her. She'd hit her mark. And hard.

Cold anger radiated off him, and she bit her lip and swallowed against the bitter lump in her throat. The lie had been ridiculous, but effective. There was no other man in her head, and he probably assumed she'd meant Kenneth. Though the last person she'd ever imagine while seeking her own pleasure would be Kenneth. That would kill her arousal on the spot.

Clint climbed off her and a moment later she heard him leave the tent. She drew in a ragged breath, already regretting her harsh words.

But the idea Clint had slept with her—even partly—to distract her from Kenneth cut deep. Sliced right through her trust and their friendship.

Tears burned her eyes, even as she told herself it was better this way. They never should have slept together. Maybe now he'd back off. Because that's what she wanted. Right? To never be anything but friends?

Her heart twisted and she already knew the answer.

Chapter Twelve

Clint jerked upright and blinked groggily. He glanced over at Allie, still sleeping with her back to him. He checked his watch and his brows rose in dismay.

Jeez, had he really slept that late? He'd been tossing and turning half the night before falling into a light sleep just as the sun had started to rise.

Climbing out of his sleeping bag, he left the tent and strode to the lake's edge to wash up then went to build a fire. His body had a subtle ache in it and his head a light throb, likely from stress and having slept like shit last night.

Moving through the quiet campsite, his jaw clenched as he remembered the hateful little taunt Allie had thrown at him right after they'd had sex. A taunt that had slid straight through his heart like a knife through soft butter.

He crunched some newspaper in the makeshift fire pit and laid some kindling down. Crouching down, he lit a match and held it to the paper, watching it catch fire.

Not like he could really blame her for the venomous words though. He'd completely stuck his foot in his mouth with that little comment about her not thinking about Ken's wedding. Hell, how had he let that come out? No matter whether or not he'd been thinking it.

And Allie had been hurt. The way her soft, curvy body had tensed beneath him. So she'd thrown out that vicious response. Part of him knew her words had been a deliberate lie to hurt him. They had to be. How long had she denied a lingering interest in Kenneth?

He stood again and walked down the lake, shoving a hand through his hair.

But now there it was. A tiny seed of doubt that maybe there was a ring of truth in her words. A doubt that had his stomach clenching and the bitter burn of jealousy in his throat.

Why should he be jealous? Why should he even care? Damn, she should have been out of his system now. He'd slept with her. Goal accomplished. This fervent need to have her that had been in his blood for years should've been extinguished. Just like any other woman he went to bed with. Sure there was the initial desire, but generally after one night the itch was scratched.

So why was it different with Allie?

His cock twitched beneath his jeans. The memory of how she'd looked before he'd left the tent this morning flitted through his head. She'd been snuggled deep into the sleeping bag, curled up into fetal position. Her lips moist and parted. God he'd wanted her. Again. And he hated that weakness within himself.

He turned away from the lake and walked back to the fire, now crackling and smoking in the early morning dawn.

Allison wasn't out of his system. Far from it.

The zipper on the tent sounded and he turned to see her climbing out. She kept her gaze lowered—a towel wrapped around her slender body as she strode across the site toward him.

He found himself hoping she would kiss him, whisper good morning. Hmm. What an asinine fantasy.

Instead she moved right past him to kneel down and grab the bottle of cleanser out of the duffle bag by the chair.

Clint's gaze caught on the naked globes of her ass, peeking out from under the towel. God in heaven. His dick jumped to attention and the air sucked from his lungs.

She stood and turned around. He lifted his gaze, but she'd already caught him looking.

Her mouth thinned, her cheeks turned pink again. "Do you have to ogle me?"

"I've done a hell of lot more than ogle you, Allie."

Her eyes flashed. "Fuck you."

"Is that another invitation?"

He watched the tension invade her body and her gaze turned hard.

"No. It wasn't an invitation. And don't count on getting into my pants again—the first time was a fluke. Now if you'll excuse me I need to go wash the smell of sex-that-never-should've-happened off me."

Her eyes narrowed and mouth tight, she swept toward the lake.

He caught her wrist before she could move past him.

"It should've happened. And it'll happen again," he promised before he could stop himself and reached his thumb out to trace her bottom lip. "And next time when I'm inside you, I'll make damn sure my name is the only one you're calling out in your head."

Her cheeks flushed and something close to regret flickered in her gaze. Then she tugged free and scowled.

"Like I said, don't count on it."

He watched as she ran to the lake's edge and dropped the towel before wading into the water.

Her shrill scream swept over the vast lake and into the canopy of trees.

"Gah, this is insane." She dunked underwater and then surfaced, squeezing the soap into the palm of her hand.

She sure did bathe a lot. Clint jerked his gaze away from her lush curves, his blood pounding harder. Not that he was complaining with such a great view.

He swallowed hard and winced. Damn. Maybe he was getting a bit of a sore throat.

He strode over to the SUV and grabbed a bottle of water out of the back, downing half of it in one swallow. His fingers crunched around the plastic bottle and he used the back of his hand to wipe across his forehead.

His brows drew together and he lowered the water back down to his side uneasily. No. It couldn't be. He hadn't felt hot. His skin had probably just retained some of the heat from the fire. Of course. That was all.

He grabbed the muffins from the car, another couple of bottles of water, then turned to head back to the fire.

Allison had left the lake and gone back into the tent. The sounds of her getting dressed and cursing about being cold could easily be heard.

He sank back into the chair, just as the ache in his body seemed to intensify. Hell, he should've made himself attempt to get more sleep this morning.

Maybe food would help. He pried open the container of muffins and lifted two out. Leaning forward, he set one on Allison's chair and kept one for himself.

"I'm starving."

His gaze lifted to where she'd just emerged from the tent. She'd put on jeans today with the long-sleeved black shirt.

"Coffee ready?" she asked, sitting down and picking up her muffin. "Hmm. No bacon today?"

"No." He unwrapped his muffin and broke off a piece. "If you want coffee, you'll have to make it."

She sighed. "Shall I give you a foot massage as well?"

The muffin was tasteless in his mouth, but he forced down the bite.

"I'd prefer a full body."

"I bet you would." She grabbed the bottle of water he'd handed her and unscrewed the cap. "I don't need any coffee. I'll just drink this."

He nodded in response, finding it easier just not to talk. Skipping the coffee was probably a good thing. The acidity would just aggravate his throat further.

"What are we going to do today? Another hike? More canoeing?"

He gave a half shrug and took another bite of muffin. Hell, going back to sleep was starting to sound like a great idea.

"You know," her tone held the slightest bit of suspicion, "you're not acting like yourself."

Unable to force down any more of the muffin, he put it on the ground and closed his eyes again. The wave of dizziness didn't ease, just seemed to intensify.

He heard her stand up.

"Okay, well, whatever. You're going to ignore me. Fine. You know, I think I'm going to take a walk."

He lifted one eyelid and gave her a look of disbelief.

"What?" She lifted her hands and shrugged. "I've gotta use the bathroom, okay? Or, sorry, the ground."

He waved her off, and closed his eyes again. His head pounded harder and his throat had begun to hit the difficult to swallow stage. Damn it. There'd be no more denying it. He was sick.

With an inward curse—since it hurt to even breathe, let alone talk—he hoped like hell whatever had infected him would pass quickly.

Allison cast a quick glance at the campsite and ran her hand over the pocket of her jeans.

Relief mingled with the rapid pounding of her heart when she felt the slight bulge of Clint's cell phone. Thank God she'd thought to slip it into her jeans after her morning swim.

Clint was nearly slumped over in his seat when she looked at him again. Her brows drew together and a spark of concern lit inside her, but she quickly brushed it aside.

"This is the chance you've been waiting for," she muttered to herself. "You have to find an open area to get a signal."

She needed to get away from Clint. After last night she couldn't stay any longer with him or she'd risk losing more than just her inhibitions to him. She'd lose her heart. His little comment had hurt. Much, much more than it should have.

Allison pushed on through the trees and ignored the prickle of fear at the thought of the wild animals they'd seen yesterday. Once she found a clearing in the trees, she pulled the phone from her pocket and flipped it open.

Her gaze looked on the bars of service available. Nothing yet. Maybe she needed to get to higher ground? She plunged through onward, desperate to get at least one bar. One bar meant she could call someone. Anyone. Definitely not Leah again, though. That little witch had turned against—there!

She gasped and dug her toes into the earth, stumbling another couple of steps before she jerked to a rough stop.

A bar. There was one—damn it! It was gone. She groaned and took a couple of steps backward, lifting the phone higher into the air. There it was again.

Keeping her arm raised, she hit the button to access Clint's phone book and scrolled through it. She saw Ken's name and hesitated, drawing her bottom lip between her teeth. Hmm. It might be a bit crazy, but then he could just be the smartest choice.

The man could maybe talk some sense into his completely nutty kidnapping friend. Completely amazing in bed kidnapping—*stop it.*

Before she could talk herself out of it, she hit dial and stood on her tiptoes to bring her mouth closer to the phone. She didn't dare lower it in case she lost that one bar.

The ringing came through unsteady and weak, but she heard it. Her pulse jumped and her muscles tensed with the hope that he'd answer.

The ringing stopped before there was silence. Had she lost the signal?

"Clint? Is that you, buddy?"

She heard his voice and squealed, "Ken?"

"*Allison?*" His voice came across crackly, but the confusion in his tone was obvious. "What are you doing on Clint's phone?"

"Kenneth. I need a favor. Can you send someone—?"

"What? Allison, you're breaking up. Where are you?"

"*Fuck.* I'm in the woods. The goddamn woods with Clint, our forest ranger friend."

"What? All I heard was 'fuck a forest ranger' or something. You're cutting out like crazy. Look, can you call me back when you get better recepti—"

"Don't you dare hang up! Clint has kidnapped me to keep me from talking to you. Did you hear me? You need to send someone to come pick me up out here."

"I can't—did you say he—"

"Montana. He took me to some bear-ridden forest in Montana."

"*Allie?*"

The hoarse male cry came from nearby in the woods. Allison slammed the phone shut and stuffed it back in her pocket, scowling. Had Kenneth even heard *any* of that?

"Hold on, I'm still going to the bathroom," she yelled.

She heard his footsteps halt and she waited a few seconds before clearing her throat.

"Okay, here I come." She strode back into the forest, forcing a smile onto her face.

Clint leaned against the trunk of a tree, looking pale and maybe even a little weak. Her brows drew together and she slowed her stride. Was he getting sick?

"What were you doing?" he rasped.

"I told you. I was going to the bathroom."

His head moved from side to side and his gaze narrowed. "I could have sworn you were talking to someone."

"Oh that," she waved her hand and moved past him back toward the campsite, "there was this deer nearby watching me pee. I told it to back the hell off before I shot it and had it hung above my fireplace."

She held her breath, hoping he didn't suspect she'd been on the phone. But how could he? She bit her lip, increasing her stride. She'd just have to put his cell phone back into the SUV when he wasn't watching.

The fire was still going when she sat back down into the chair. Her pulse had yet to slow as she let her tongue sweep across her dry lips.

Clint entered the campsite again, lagging behind longer than she'd first thought.

He stopped in front of the fire and stared down at it, his gaze unfocused and unblinking.

"Clint?" she prodded hesitantly. "Are you okay?"

"Fine. Just fine." His voice was scratchy. "Though, I'm going to lie down in the tent for a minute."

"Umm...okay." She lifted one eyebrow.

He stared at the fire another minute, before he blinked.

"Right. Lie down." His head nodded a bit sluggishly up and down. "Be back...in a few."

"Okay." She tilted her head and watched him stumble back into the tent.

He didn't bother to zip it and a second later she heard him collapse onto the mattress.

Hmm. This was interesting. She tapped her foot on the ground and glanced around the campsite. Too bad they were miles from civilization, or she'd consider trying to hike out on foot.

She sighed and looked out over the lake. Canoeing had been fun yesterday. Maybe she should give it a try again. Alone.

Visions of the boat flipping and her being tossed into the frigid water, only to be snatched up by some bear who happened to be swimming across the lake flickered through her head. Hmm. No, solid ground sounded much safer.

She glanced back at the tent and frowned. It was too quiet. He must really be out.

She stood and moved hesitantly toward the flap to the tent. Lifting it up, she peeked at the bed.

Clint lay on his stomach, his arms spread out and his head turned to the side on the pillow facing away from her. She stepped into the tent, telling herself she just wanted to grab a sweater. She moved right to the edge of the bed and knelt down beside him.

His face was flushed and his forehead had beads of sweat across it. His lips were parted and the breaths escaping came in shallow gasps.

She drew her bottom lip between her teeth and placed her hand against his forehead. Jeez. He was burning up.

Rocking back on her heels, she gave him a considering glance. Had he known he was coming down with something when he'd kidnapped her? And how long had he been this sick?

Realization hit a second later. Shit. Had *she* gotten him sick? She glanced back down at him and made a tally of his symptoms. The tension eased from her shoulders and she sighed. He probably had the same damn thing she'd just gotten over.

The air whistled out from between her clenched teeth and she shook her head. It was a doozy too.

She took a few steps backward. This *so* wasn't her problem. Whatever happened to him now was nothing but karma. She'd just go out and throw another log on the campfire, then sit to enjoy the view.

She turned to leave the tent and tripped over his jeans. The familiar jingle of keys sent a tingle of awareness down her spine. Keys. Those couldn't possibly be the keys to the SUV, could they?

She cast him another quick glance to ensure he was still asleep, then crouched down to dig through the pockets of his jeans. Sliding her finger into a metal loop, she pulled the keys from the denim slowly.

Her eyes widened and her pulse took off as she recognized the key to his vehicle.

Oh God. Could she do it? Just get the hell in the car and drive off? Her heart skipped a beat. But Clint was sick. That would be wrong.

He kidnapped you and possibly slept with you just to take your mind off Kenneth's wedding. Take the keys and go. You can send help for him later.

On a split-second decision, she listened to her inner voice and ignored her conscience. She hurried out of the tent, sprinting toward his SUV.

Once inside she shut the door and locked it. She glanced back at the tent, the blood roaring through her veins. Her mouth dried out.

She struggled against the hesitation that again flared up. He'd freak out when he figured out she'd left.

Allison tugged open the glove compartment and pulled out an old receipt and a pen. She scrawled a harried *I'm going home, but I'll send someone in the nearest town back to get you* on the receipt and hesitated. What if he'd discovered she'd left already? It was risky to run it back. But she couldn't just drive off without leaving him a clue to where she went. If he'd been a random kidnapper, sure. But this was Clint. They'd been friends since they were kids.

She unlocked the door and pulled the handle, sliding back out of the SUV. Her feet hit the ground with a thud before she tiptoed back to the campsite.

Instead of going back into the tent—because she would not be *that* stupid—she set the receipt on his chair and placed a big rock on top of it.

A loud, raspy cough erupted from inside the tent and she froze, choking back a startled gasp. *Please fall back asleep. Please fall back asleep.*

"Allie?"

Shit.

"Please...bring me a water?" he asked weakly.

What could she do? Grab him a water and run like hell? No. That wouldn't work.

"Allie?"

She'd hesitated too long. The sound of him stumbling off the bed could clearly be heard.

Go. With a barely audible groan she took off at a run toward the SUV again.

"Allie—"

His voice cut off as she jumped in and slammed the door to his vehicle. She tossed a water bottle out the window so he would at least have that, then jammed the keys into the ignition.

The engine roared to life and she slammed the gear into drive. Clint's hand slapped against the back window and she yelped, hitting the gas. Dirt flew as the SUV shot out of the camping site.

Her gaze lifted to the rearview mirror and she watched as Clint took a few steps after her before collapsing to his knees in the dirt.

"Oh, come on," she yelled. "That's a little dramatic, don't you think?"

Still, guilt twisted her stomach into a painful knot and she jerked her gaze back to the road, even though she was close to hitting the brakes.

You're not a camper, she reminded herself. She was never here willingly, and damn it she had nothing to feel guilty about. Absolutely nothing.

She focused again on the narrow dirt road that the SUV moved down. She eased up on the gas pedal, the constant bouncing inside the vehicle clearly an indication this was a road you didn't want to go too fast down.

Once she'd slowed down to less than twenty miles per hour, the ride wasn't quite as rough.

She stared at the road ahead of her, wishing she'd been awake when Clint had first taken her out to the campsite. Because where the hell she was God only knew.

Images of Clint on his knees on the earthy ground of the campsite flashed in her head. He'd looked pitiful. So helpless.

She drew in an unsteady breath as her throat tightened.

And this was just the first day of his symptoms. When she'd had it the nasty stuff hadn't hit until about the second day. At that point she'd been pretty much incapacitated. Which meant Clint would pretty much be screwed in the morning.

But it wasn't like she was ditching him completely. She'd send help. He'd be fine.

Swallowing the lump of guilt in her throat, she clenched her fingers tighter around the steering wheel and pressed down harder on the gas.

Chapter Thirteen

He was going to die. Alone and sick, on the hard ground of this campsite.

Clint's knees shook and he fell to the side, sprawling out on the dirt floor. He breathed in the earthy, familiar sent of nature before his nostrils clogged and his sinuses started to throb. His throat burned and dizziness swirled in his head.

It had finally happened. She'd stolen his SUV to run home to Kenneth. And now he was going to die.

He never got sick. Never. Rolling his head to the side, he gauged the distance between him and the tent, whimpering like a damn puppy.

One thing was certain. He couldn't very well pass out right here on the ground. He'd likely end up bitten by a dozen mosquitoes—or maybe like Allie had feared—eaten by a ravenous bear.

With a groan he pulled himself to his feet and took a small step toward the tent. He spotted a piece of paper on one of the chairs and stumbled over to read it. Cursing, he tossed it into the fire and made his way back to the tent. Sweat beaded on his brow and nausea rolled through him.

He ground his teeth together and forced himself to take another step. He reached the tent and leaned down to climb inside. Another rage of thirst swept through him and he gave a weak curse. Damn. She'd tossed him a bottle of water, but he hadn't grabbed it.

His gaze shifted to the chair near the fire and he spotted a half drunk bottle. How come he hadn't seen that thirty seconds ago?

It was only about twenty feet away, but it might as well have been a few miles.

He sighed and moved into the tent, just barely making it the few steps to the bed before he collapsed again onto the mattress.

The scent of Allison tickled his nostrils and he closed his eyes, realizing his head rested on her pillow.

She'd left him. His lips twitched weakly, but it was hard to find the energy to be amused. Not that he was really surprised she'd up and left. More that he hadn't been able to stop her. If he hadn't been so damn sick it never would have happened. She wouldn't have gotten within two feet of his SUV with his keys. But she had. And now she was gone.

The pulsing ache in his body intensified. He groaned aloud, a long and pitiful sound that sounded more like a frog getting strangled.

He closed his eyes and waited for the oblivion of sleep to overtake him. Finally, it happened.

When he woke later, it was dark outside. His brows drew together as he tried to discover what had woken him.

The sound of shuffling came from outside the tent and he froze. Christ. Maybe it *was* a bear. He hadn't even cleaned up the muffin he'd left on the ground after breakfast.

More clanging sounded and he groaned and managed to prop himself up on the bed. Definitely a bear, he decided. Then came the high-pitched, "*Shit.*"

His blood slowed, before speeding right back up.

"Allie?" Her name on his lips was barely audible, even to him. There was no way she could have heard him.

He lay back on the blankets and waited, staring at the canopy of the tent and wishing to God the pounding in his head would subside.

Before long the tent flap lifted and the beam of a flashlight honed in on him. He blinked, his pupils burning from the bright light.

"Hey," he croaked. "Watch the light—"

"Good. You're awake. Get your butt out of bed and into the back of SUV."

He struggled to sit up again. "What?"

"I can't very well tear down the tent with you inside it, so get out."

"You want to tear down—"

"God, you sound like you've been gargling nails." She sighed and climbed into the tent.

He gave a soft grunt, the effort to talk too much again.

Allison reached his side then leaned down to take his arm and help him off the bed.

Embarrassed by his own weakness, he just barely resisted the urge to snarl that he didn't need her help. But damn it, he did.

In the dark their gazes met and held.

"You came back," he finally managed to ask. "Why?"

She lowered her lashes and harrumphed. "Because even if you did kidnap me and take me *camping*, I still have a fucking conscience. Now let's just get you back into the car so I can get this campsite torn down."

"Do you know how?"

"I'll figure it out. Stop talking. I can barely understand you and I know it hurts like hell."

Really? And how the hell did she know that? The snarky reply had to make do in his head since it would have drained him to make it aloud.

With her help they moved across the campsite to his SUV, which she'd backed up almost to the fire pit.

She tugged open the back door and tossed a pillow in on the seat.

"Lie down on the seat and make yourself comfortable. Hopefully this will only take a few minutes."

He grabbed her wrist, weak in his movements, but it still halted her from leaving.

"Water?" he begged.

She gave a slight nod then pulled away, moving around back to grab him a water. She quickly twisted off the lid and handed him the lukewarm bottle.

He downed it easily in a few swallows before falling back against the pillow.

"I'll be back shortly," she muttered and turned away.

Disbelief mixed with self-pity as he watched her through the open door. Before his eyes she took apart the campsite. Deflated the bed, folded it up and hauled it back to the SUV. Then went back, jerking up stakes and getting the tent down.

Hmm. And this from a woman who'd never camped in her adult life. Probably fifteen minutes passed before she climbed into the driver's seat and started the engine.

"You'll have to come back for the canoe. I wasn't about to try and get that loaded onto your car."

He cleared his throat and winced at the resulting pain. "Where are we—?"

"To your place. So don't fall asleep, because your ass needs to tell me exactly where we're going."

The vehicle swerved to the left as she narrowly missed a deer sprinting across the road.

"Damn animals are road hazards," she muttered.

His chest bounced with a silent laugh and he closed his eyes, drowsy again.

"Don't you go to sleep on me."

He opened his eyes and looked up. Her gaze stared back at him in the rearview mirror.

"I mean it. I have no idea how to get out of this overgrown park."

His mouth tightened. Which was probably why she'd come back for him in the first place.

"Not like that's why I came back for you."

Right. Then what were her reasons? Sympathy? Ha. More like guilt.

"I just," she cleared her throat. "Didn't much care for the idea of getting slapped with a manslaughter charge."

She thought he would have died out there? He tilted his head and gave a slight nod. Well, actually, he'd begun to think he'd die out there with the way he felt.

"Not like you actually would have died. But, yeah." She sighed. "How far away from your house are we?"

He opened his mouth to answer.

"No, don't talk. Use your fingers. How many hours?"

He held up one finger.

"Okay. That's not so bad." She pushed a hand through her hair. "I'll stop off at a convenience station or something before we get there."

He shook his head, wondering if she would even see him.

Her gaze lifted. "What? There is a gas station or something, right?"

He kept shaking his head.

"How much further is one of those?"

Pursing his lips, he debated how to say fifteen minutes past his house without moving his lips.

"Oh never mind. We can figure it out in the morning."

He sat up slightly and looked around. "Turn right."

"What? Where?" she looked around.

"There," he croaked, pointing to a small turn off barely visible.

She slowed the SUV down and turned onto the road. Satisfied that she'd obeyed him without hesitation, he relaxed again, making himself comfortable to guide her the rest of the way to his house.

By the time they reached his place it had to be close to ten.

He sat up from the backseat, the effort double what it should have been. His back ached from the position he'd forced himself into, and his head throbbed something fierce.

"This is it?" She turned off the engine and sat staring at his house in silence.

He gave a short nod. What was she thinking? That it looked like some hillbilly log cabin in the middle of nowhere? He grimaced as he pulled open the door and slid out. But then maybe his home was somewhat a mix of that.

The two-story home was essentially an overgrown log cabin, and it was fifteen miles to the nearest town.

"No bright streetlight to help me get you inside either," she grumbled and climbed out after him.

He shook his head and limped toward the front door.

"Hang on." She rushed after him and grabbed his arm. "The last thing I want you doing is falling over from exhaustion."

He gave her a fierce scowl, even as he let her absorb some of his weight. The soft curve of her breast rubbed against his arm as the familiar scent of her tickled his nostrils—well, the one that wasn't plugged.

"Which one is your house key?" She held up his key ring to him.

Clint plucked it from her hand, locating the one that would open his front door.

She took it back and fumbled to get it in the door. He grimaced, realizing he should've done it. In the dark she was pretty much doing everything by touch.

"There we go." She twisted the knob and pushed open the door. Her hand moved over the wall until she found the switch and flipped it up, soft light flooded the room.

"Where's your bedroom?"

His lips curled and he turned to her with a raised eyebrow.

"Okay, you're sick." She got up in his face and glared. "Stop thinking about sex for one minute, would you?"

He gave a half shrug and pointed.

"I have to get you up those stairs?" Her eyes widened and she glanced toward the spiraling wood staircase against the far wall.

Irritation finally pricked. Why had she insisted on helping him out if she was going to bitch the entire time?

176

"I can get up the stairs myself." Just saying the sentence left his throat raw and hoarse, but it did a little something for his pride.

He brushed off her arm and made his way toward the stairs himself.

"No, Clint, I'm sorry. Hang on."

With a wave of dismissal, he took the first step up to the bedroom loft on the second floor.

"Okay, umm," she sighed, "I'll make you some tea."

Halfway up the steps, his gaze drifted down to her. Tea? Did he even have tea? And if he did would he honestly drink it?

"Beer?" he countered hoarsely.

"I am *not* getting you a damn beer," she shouted in disbelief. "You're sick and you want beer? *Argh.* Get your butt in bed before I give it the kicking it deserves."

He sighed and forced himself up the last few steps. Beer had sounded pretty good, actually. The alcohol might have had a numbing affect on his throat.

After tugging his T-shirt over his head, he pushed down his jeans and kicked them to the floor, naked now except for his boxers. The effort of undressing drained what little energy he had left, and he stumbled the last few feet to his bed.

Collapsing onto the mattress, he dragged a blanket over him, surprised at how cold he suddenly was.

His eyelids fluttered a few times, before he gave in and just let them close.

He must have drifted off into sleep because the next thing he knew Allison was gently touching his shoulder.

"Hey," she said softly when his lids opened again.

He gave a weak nod in response.

Her brows drew together in a frown and she lowered a hand to his forehead.

"You're burning up."

The concern in her hazel eyes tugged at his gut and weakened him emotionally a little. Made him want to give in to the miserable bug that had invaded his body and encourage Allison's sympathy for him. His inner eight-year-old was suddenly ripe and ready to be nurtured.

"You look terrible." She shook her head and tried to remove her hand, but he caught her wrist, not ready to lose that contact. "Please, let me get you some Tylenol or something."

"In a minute," he rasped. "Please. Stay."

Reluctance and hesitation flickered in her gaze, "First take a sip of tea."

She held the mug in front of his lips.

He scowled, but obediently blew on the steaming liquid before taking a small sip.

"One more."

He glared at her.

"Come on, or I leave."

Control freak. He held her gaze and drank another sip, then patted the mattress next to him.

She sighed, looked around the room, as if trying to figure out a way out of this, then sat down.

He scooted over to make more room for her on the queen-sized bed. She slid further in and sat up with her back propped against the wood carved headboard.

Without realizing that he was even moving, he moved his head onto her lap. Allison's hand smoothed back his hair and she sighed.

"I shouldn't have said what I did last night," he rasped. "About the wedding. I'm sorry."

She stilled in her movements of smoothing his hair and he closed his eyes, wondering what she was thinking. Just getting the apology out had literally hurt like hell.

"It's all right. I acted pretty shitty too," she said softly.

Relief swept through him, but he didn't answer. Was too busy trying not to think about the softness of her thigh and how close his face was to her—

"Clint."

"Hmm?" was all he managed to grunt in response.

"Never mind..." Her fingers slid upward and into his hair. "You have soft hair. Great guy hair."

Great guy hair? Women thought about men's hair that much? Hell, men didn't think about men's hair that much, did they? Or maybe that was just him.

"I really should get you those meds, Clint."

"Stay." His fingers curled into her jeans and he pressed his head harder against her. As if the weight of his head alone could keep her pinned down.

She didn't move though. He could sense the tension that had filtered into her body slowly ease again.

"Go to sleep, Clint. I'll stay until you pass out." She resumed stroking his forehead. "Then I'm going downstairs and watching that big ass TV hanging on your wall."

His chest bounced with a silent laugh.

"I wouldn't think you'd want some big flat screen in your house if you're such an outdoors guy. But you know what they say...boys and their toys."

Pretty much. Wait until she discovered his Wii. He didn't play it all that often, but some days he needed a little entertainment since he was so isolated out here.

"You asleep yet?"

He lifted his head and gave her an incredulous look.

She made a face and laughed. "I'm talking too much, aren't I?"

He arched an eyebrow and nodded.

"Fine. I'll shut up. But you go to sleep. My legs are going to cramp." She yawned.

Lowering his head back to her lap, he almost wished for that Tylenol. His throat had gone raw and his head still pounded. But that would mean Allison would have to get up and his face would be planted back on the pillow instead of her soft thigh.

His lips twitched. Screw the pills. He closed his eyes, knowing he wouldn't be able to fall asleep. It didn't matter. He could fake it and enjoy the moment.

Allison could tell the minute he finally passed out. The fingers that had been gripping her jeans relaxed and his breathing evened out. It only took a few minutes really, and truth be told she was a little bummed to scoot him off her.

He didn't even stir, just settled against the pillow she placed his head on.

She slid off the bed and wrapped her arms around her waist, staring down at him. Hearing him apologize for his comment after they'd made love was such a relief. Lifted a huge weight off her heart.

You're too easy.

Shaking her head, she turned and walked back down the spiral staircase to the downstairs. Her gaze drifted around the house and she drew in a sigh of content. Gorgeous. This house was straight out of some backwoods living magazine or something. So cozy and homey, and yet furnished with all the comfort and technology you'd expect to see in a bachelor pad.

She went to sit on the leather couch and grabbed the remote off of the coffee table. After turning on the TV she flipped through the channels until she found a makeover reality show that looked somewhat interesting.

Five minutes later, she flipped channels again, appalled at the garbage some networks were putting out nowadays.

She settled on watching the news, mainly because it was boring enough to make her drowsy. Her gaze shifted to the time at the bottom of the news program and she yawned. Eleven.

Grabbing the fleece throw resting over the back of the couch, she pulled it over her body and snuggled deeper into the cushions of the couch.

Her eyelids fluttered, once, then twice. Finally she gave up trying to pretend she cared about the latest pop star's demise and let them stay shut.

A loud crash woke her. She jerked upright, her heart fluttering in her chest. What the hell had that been?

From the stairway came a slow groan and she kicked the blanket off her legs, lurching off the couch.

"What are you doing out of bed?" she scoffed and hurried up the stairs to where Clint sat on his butt.

"Thirsty."

She grasped his elbow with an exasperated sigh. "But I left you tea."

181

"Drank—ouch—" he winced and touched his throat, "—it already."

"All right. I'll get you some water, but for the love of God, please stay in bed, already, will you?"

He gave the barest hint of a nod.

After a little more effort than she cared for, she finally got him back into bed.

"I thought—" he swallowed and winced, "—you'd left me."

He stared up at her with mournful eyes that could have been set on a stray dog. Pathetic and pleading. *Endearing and adorable in a sexy way.*

"If I were going to leave you, then I would have done it when I took your SUV." She placed her hands on her hips and blew a strand of hair out of her eye. "But obviously I came back."

His chest puffed up and the pathetic puppy look shifted to something hotter and possessive.

Her pulse sped up and she drew in a quick breath. "I'll go get that water."

Before he could say anything else or give her another look that made her panties melt, she spun on her heels and raced back down the stairs.

Her hand trembled as she filled a glass full of water. Good Lord this man affected her. No man had ever had this kind of power over her. The power to make her knees weak and her heart race as if she'd run a mile.

Clint had made love to her in a way no other man past or present would be able to equal. And the idea freaked her out more than a little.

She clenched her fists and drew in an unsteady breath. *Stop thinking about it.*

Spying a box of saltine crackers on the counter, she stopped to grab a handful. He would probably be getting hungry. Had he even eaten since this morning?

She had. She'd taken out the rest of the granola bars in the backseat when she'd first stolen his car. Then the guilt had kicked it, proved too much to resist, and she'd turned around to go get him.

After a brief search of the cupboards turned up a tray, she placed the water and crackers on it and set off up the stairs again.

She half expected him to be passed out in the bed when she arrived. Instead, he laid semi reclined against the pillows, his gaze focused on the stairs as she entered the loft.

Relief flickered in his gaze and she felt another stab of guilt. He really expected her to run and leave him. But then she really couldn't blame him. Maybe he figured that since she'd gotten him back to his place, she would have a clear conscience to bail.

And technically you could.

She squelched back the voice of reason and walked toward the bed, setting the tray down on the mattress.

"Thank you," he whispered and grabbed the glass from her.

She watched as he tilted the glass back and drank with obvious thirst. Her gaze lowered to his neck and the muscles that moved as he swallowed.

A drop of water slid past his lips and rolled off his chin, landing with a splat onto his naked chest.

She swallowed hard, her gaze focused on the brown nipples just beneath the smattering of chest hair. A vision flickered in her head. An image of her straddling him, her hair brushing his chest as she leaned down to flick her tongue over the small nipples.

Desire stirred low in her belly and she bit back a groan.

You're ridiculous, Allison. The man is sick and you're thinking dirty thoughts.

She shook her head and bit back a snort.

The crunching of a cracker snapped her attention back to him. He'd picked up a saltine and eaten half.

"Don't go back to the couch."

She lifted her gaze to his and saw the determination in them. The words had hurt his throat. It had been evident in the raw tone and tight expression on his face.

"Clint, you're sick," she said softly.

He ate the last half of the cracker, but didn't look away from her. After he'd swallowed and taken another sip of water, he patted the bed.

She sighed and rolled her eyes, even as her heart fluttered like a restrained butterfly in her chest. Damn it. This was getting ridiculous.

"Clint..."

He caught her hand and tugged her forward. She stumbled the few steps until her knees bumped into the frame of the bed.

"Stay."

He propped himself up and she suddenly found herself well within easy reach of him.

Using two fingers, he tugged at the waistband of the jeans he'd bought her. It was a light tug, but had enough momentum to make her surrender and sit down on the mattress.

He urged her down onto her back and she laid her head on the pillow, while he remained propped up above her.

"Clint..."

His fingers moved to her mouth, cutting off her words of protest.

She obediently pressed her lips together and bit back a sigh at the rough texture of his fingertips.

He moved his hand downward, over the swell of her breast then onto the plane of her stomach. His fingers stopped at the waistband of her jeans and this time she was unable to stop the ragged breath that escaped. Her entire body sizzled with hot awareness.

He lifted his gaze to hers as his fingers slid the button through the hole in the denim before tugging the tab of her zipper down.

She bit her lip and watched the flare of desire in his eyes.

"Off," he whispered and gave her now undone jeans another tug, leaving no doubt in her mind what he intended.

And this was why she would have been a terrible nurse. The man wasn't feeling well and needed his rest, and yet she had no intention of stopping him from pursuing whatever naughty intentions he had.

Hell no. In fact, she decided, kicking off her jeans, she had every intention of encouraging him.

Now, clothed only in the tiny thong he'd bought her and the short sleeve T-shirt, she lay back down and watched him watch her.

His murmur of approval was barely audible as he moved to lie beside her. He rolled onto his side, his lips seeking the hollow of her throat while his hand moved confidently to cup between her legs.

Her back arched and she tilted her head to allow his lips to graze the spot between her neck and shoulder.

Moisture gathered hot between her legs, the sweet ache increasing when he ground the heel of his palm against her mound.

His mouth opened over her neck and he sucked, each pull sending stabs of pleasure straight between her legs. She squirmed against him almost dizzy with desire now.

He slipped a finger beneath the silk thong and deep into her.

"Mmm." He lifted his mouth from the rapid beating pulse on her neck to claim her lips. His tongue thrust deep and he added a second finger inside her.

She matched the taunting flicks of his tongue, angling her head to deepen the kiss as he pressed her harder against the pillow.

The slick sounds of him moving his fingers in and out of her channel made her flush self-consciously. God, she was turned on. So damn hot for him. She'd never responded to another man like this.

He slipped his thumb beneath her thong as well to find her sensitized nub, the two fingers inside her still penetrating her with maddening slowness.

He rolled her own moisture over the sensitive ball of flesh and her hips jerked against him.

"Like that?" he murmured hoarsely, lifting his mouth from hers.

"Please. Oh God." She gripped his forearms, her eyes almost rolling into the back of her head as her nails dug into his skin.

He added more pressure with his thumb and stroked his fingers along the wall of her channel.

Allison panted, bucking against his hand as incoherent pleas spilled from her lips.

His mouth descended to capture hers again, just as he hit all the right spots at once.

Her body went taut, her calves tightened and her toes curled. The choked gasp she made was caught up in the kiss, swept away with his tongue.

Nearly a minute must have passed before the trembling subsided from her weak muscles. Several minutes before coherent thought entered her head again.

Clint fell back on the bed, looking as weak and out of breath as she felt.

Guilt twisted in her gut and she pressed a hand against her own hot forehead. Only hers was hot because he'd made her hot, not because she was fighting off some God-awful virus.

"Clint?" She sat upright, smoothed the hair back from his forehead.

He groaned and made a weak effort to push her hand away.

"What? What's wrong? Do you feel sicker?"

He reached for the sheet and pulled it up over his waist, but not before she'd spotted the sizeable erection he sported.

She grinned and ran a hand over his chest. "We can do something about that you know."

He grimaced and shook his head. "Can't," he whispered. "I can barely move."

Her smile turned mischievous and she laughed softly. "You don't have to move, Clint. You just need to sit there and let me take you in my mouth."

His chest rose visibly and held. When she lifted her gaze to his, his pupils were dilated and his mouth had tightened.

He'd just given her the most delicious orgasm and now was going to try to fall asleep with a raging hard-on? Wasn't that a form of torture in some countries?

She tugged the sheet down, even as he reached out to try and stop her.

"Really, Clint." She ran her finger over his erection, straining against the fabric of his boxers and said softly, "It's my turn."

"You don't—"

"I *want* to." She looked at him again and ran her tongue over her lips. "Just lie back and think of England."

He gave a weak laugh that turned into a cough, but made no further effort to push her away.

Not that she'd really expected him to. The man was in some serious discomfort.

Turning her focus back to her mission, she hooked her fingers into the elastic of his boxers and pulled them down.

His flesh slid free, proud and hard into the air, a tiny drop of moisture on the tip.

Her lips curled upward and her pulse fluttered. She hadn't tasted him yet. Hadn't gone down on him. But then the times they'd been intimate before had been a completely different ambiance. Had been hot and passionate. It was still those things, but the desperate edge was gone.

This felt softer, more sensual. Almost...loving. She didn't want to think about loving.

"Allie?" Her name was hesitant and hoarse on his lips.

She blinked and forced a slight smile. "Sorry. I was just thinking..."

He lifted an eyebrow.

Instead of going into depth about her don't-even-want-to-go-there thoughts, she settled for a more seductive response. "About how you taste."

He drew in a swift breath as she leaned over him, her hair sweeping down across his stomach.

She nuzzled his shaft, inhaling the salty muskiness of him before letting her tongue dart out to catch the drop of liquid on his tip.

Chapter Fourteen

At the first touch of her tongue, Clint was sure he would explode. His hips bucked and the air seethed out from between clenched teeth.

"Mmm. You taste good." Her breathy laughter feathered over his thigh before her tongue swept across the head of his dick again.

He squeezed his eyes shut and willed his body's response to slow down. The blood thundered through his veins, rushing south to give him the biggest damn hard-on he'd probably ever had.

Her tongue dragged up the length of his cock, before circling the head again. She paid extra attention to the tiny crease below.

"Do you want me to take you in my mouth?" she asked softly, her voice tinged with a husky naughtiness. "Take you so deep that you're stroking the back of my throat?"

Jesus. And now she was pulling out the dirty talk. As if it weren't already a guarantee he would come. But she'd figured out how much he liked it.

He opened his eyes and met her heated gaze with a slow nod.

"You do?" She didn't look away as she lowered her head and closed her mouth around the tip. She drew hard on him once, then released him with a popping sound.

His balls tightened and he bit back a groan of frustration.

Her lips curved slightly. "Do you want me to suck you until you come?"

He nodded again. Hell yeah he did. He wanted to thoroughly fuck that pretty mouth of hers, have her swallow everything when he finally exploded.

She lifted an eyebrow, almost as if to taunt him. As if she knew his thoughts.

Needing her mouth on him and unable to take any more of her teasing, he reached out and wove his fingers into her silky hair.

"How bad do you want it, Clint?"

With a growl that irritated his already sore throat, he urged her mouth back down.

She smiled and let him slide past her moist lips. Her tongue moved over his length as he slid deep into her mouth before finally brushing against the back of her throat.

He closed his eyes, his breathing uneven as he savored the feel of her mouth around him. Hot and wet, the texture of her tongue maddening against his flesh.

Still holding her hair, he pulled his hips back, drawing out slightly. Only for a moment did he tease the head of his dick against her lips before moving back into her mouth.

She found her own rhythm, following the movements of his hips and sliding her mouth up and down on him. Her soft hands reached down to fondle his balls and she started to suck harder on him.

Clint eased his fingers from her hair and relaxed against the mattress, giving her control.

She adjusted her body and the new angle brought him deeper into her mouth, down her throat.

He pressed his lips together and the air locked in his lungs with the impending climax. His balls clenched and the muscles in his body went rigid.

"Allie," he choked out her name, trying to give her a moment's warning before he came.

She didn't move away, just slowed the pace of her mouth. Then it was too late.

The guttural groan he made set his throat on fire, but the pain barely registered as he climaxed. His mind went blank as pleasure roared through his body.

He spilled himself into her willing mouth, encouraged by her moan of approval. She drew on him, sucking every last drop from him until he was empty and weak on the bed.

The soft strands of her hair trailed across his stomach as she lifted her head from him.

"See?" she murmured, drowsily. "I told you I'd take care of you."

Clint opened his eyes slowly, his breathing still heavy. That had been amazing. So damn incredible. One night with her would never be enough. Somehow he knew one year wouldn't even be.

In her gaze he read satisfaction and yet the faintest hint of doubt.

"Come here," he whispered and held out his hand.

She didn't hesitate, just climbed up the bed and lay next to him.

He tugged the covers up over them and slid his arm around her, drawing her into the curve of his body.

The rapid pounding of his heart began to slow and the tenderness for Allison he'd been trying to deny existed swelled up in his chest, making it difficult to breathe.

He brushed his lips against her forehead, squelching back the possibility he was falling for her—really falling for her. Like, ditch any pretense of just being friends, because he wanted so much more.

She snuggled closer and pressed a kiss against his chest in response.

His brows drew together as drowsiness threatened to pull him into slumber. Then again maybe he wasn't the only one falling.

Clint woke from a heavy sleep, disoriented and hurting like hell.

If he'd thought yesterday was the peak of this sickness, then he'd been ridiculously wrong. Swallowing was damn near impossible, his head pounded like there was a teenager inside it with a drum set, and every muscle in his body felt like Jell-O.

He blinked a few times, trying to focus. He was home. The night before rushed back to him at the same moment he realized the soft weight pressed against his side.

Twisting his head, he noted Allison curled up against him. Her head tucked into the crook of his arm and one of her legs thrown across his.

Memories of the erotic way she'd gone down on him—the way she'd been determined to take care of him flickered through his head.

Lord, she was lovely. So innocent and sweet looking in her sleep. And the way she'd stayed snug against him all night, he'd wager she hadn't moved from his side once.

Guilt pricked in his gut and he gave a silent sigh. He'd been selfish enough to bring her to bed with him last night, but had he even taken a moment to consider he'd probably gotten her sick now?

The poor girl. She'd be miserable when it hit her.

As if sensing he'd wakened, she stirred against him and gave a soft little moan, her breast brushed against his ribcage.

If he weren't so damn miserable, he'd probably be rock hard from the contact. But as it was he was lucky to go half-mast.

She sat up and yawned, glancing down at him. "Hey. How are you feeling?"

He winced and shook his head. The words he wanted to say were buried beneath a burning throat.

"That bad, eh?" Swinging her legs off the bed, she stood. "How far is the nearest town? I'll run and grab you some Tylenol."

He opened his mouth to protest, but she waved her hand.

"You're out. I checked last night. You have one pill left in the bottle. And trust me—you're going to need a heck of a lot more than that. You've got at least another day of this." She cleared her throat. "And maybe I'll pick up some of that throat numbing spray. This should be the worst day though."

He tilted his head and narrowed his eyes. How did she know that?

She pulled on her jeans and snapped them shut. "I was out sick for almost a week, but the totally incapacitated part is just a day or two."

Disbelief washed over him just before the realization hit. She'd already had this. He needn't have felt guilty about the possibility of passing this to her—*she'd* gotten *him* sick.

"I'm going to wear your sweater," she told him, grabbing one off the ground. When she straightened up she must have seen his expression, because she laughed. *Laughed* at him.

"Yes, Clint, I got you sick." She looked around before grabbing her shoes off the ground. "It's not like I did it on purpose...in fact you probably got it that night you cornered me outside of the restaurant." She glanced up at him. "Remember when you got right up in my face?"

His forehead furrowed with his scowl. Yes, he remembered. He remembered backing her up against her car, the soft floral scent of her perfume, and wanting to kiss her until she couldn't remember Kenneth's name. God, he'd been irritated with her. Irritated and damn turned on.

"Yeah, I was totally sick then. Totally." She gave him a sweet smile. "I almost feel sorry for you right now, but it's karma, Clint. Karma."

What was karma? His eyes widened and his mouth gaped. Was she going to just up and leave him?

"Don't worry, I'm not going to leave you. You need me," she murmured. "You're kind of like an infant when you get sick. Whimpering a lot, kind of helpless..."

Helpless? And how the hell did she keep reading his thoughts?

"Okay." She slapped her palms against her thighs and nodded. "So this town. Do I just keep driving west on the road and I'll hit it?"

He nodded a bit dumbly.

"Can I get you anything before I leave? More water? Some yogurt?"

He nodded to the water. The yogurt thing wouldn't happen—his fridge was bare. He hadn't gone to the store in a week since he'd known he'd be away for awhile.

She gave quick jerk of her head and hurried down the stairs. When she returned a few minutes later she carried another glass of water and the package of crackers.

"Wow, you really need groceries. I'll grab some stuff while I'm in town." She set the items on the table next to his bed and sat beside him. "Will you be okay?"

Again he gave a dumb nod. Was he really just about to let her take his keys and drive off into town?

She leaned forward and kissed his forehead. "You'll be fine. I'll be back shortly."

He watched her stand up again and head back downstairs. "And I placed that last Tylenol in with the bag of crackers. You'll want to take it. Just sleep all morning if you can. And I took the cash from your wallet to pay for the groceries."

A moment later the front door closed, followed soon after by the roar of his SUV coming to life.

He glanced at the tray and frowned at the last pill. Well, hell. Hopefully it did the job.

Allison steered the SUV down the quiet road and stifled another yawn. First off, she needed some coffee.

She scowled and pushed her hair away from her face. And what were the chances she'd find an espresso stand in town—let alone a decent one. Of course, at this rate half decent would do.

A small gas station was the first hint at the small town Clint had told her about.

She drove past, hoping there would be more stores to follow. Not even a minute later she got her wish.

There was a nice-sized grocery store and scattered around it a strip mall with a few shops. The interesting thing was that they were all sans neon signs and built with wood. It was rather cute and blended right into the natural setting.

She pulled up to the grocery store—by no means a mega chain, but rather some mom and pop place—and parked the SUV.

Grabbing her purse, she climbed out and slammed the door, walking quickly into the small market.

Her mouth curved as she grabbed a cart and moved down the first aisle. The place was rather quaint. Again, not much neon. Small, but filled with all the necessary stuff.

She loaded up the cart with Tylenol, some meat and cheese, then hit the fruit and yogurt. Knowing Clint might be surviving on a simple diet the next couple of days, she grabbed a loaf of bread, more saltines and some Jell-O.

The deli in the back of the store caught her eye before she could make it to the register. She'd just look.

Her gaze drifted over the options they had. She spotted the wrapped sandwich and her eyes widened. The thing was huge and stacked full of meat, cheese and condiments.

After camping food, her mouth watered. She scooped it up and tossed it into the cart. Heck, at least she had a ready-to-go lunch now.

She moved toward the register again, but this time got waylaid in the freezer section. Ice cream would probably feel great on Clint's throat.

"This is ridiculous," she scoffed quietly. She shouldn't spoil the man.

With a sigh she jerked open the freezer and grabbed a carton of vanilla.

Now it was time to pay.

She got into the checkout line just as the door to the store swung open and an older woman strode in. Her narrowed eyes swept across the aisles before she strode across the front of the store.

Allison eyed the woman curiously as the checker rang her up. Obviously the woman was searching for someone.

"Did you find everything you needed, ma'am?"

She glanced back to the checker and smiled. "I did, thanks."

The young boy, probably sixteen if barely, nodded and grinned. "Do you live in town? Or just passing through?"

Hmm. How did she answer that one? *Passing through on the tail end of being kidnapped?*

"I'm just...passing through. Sure. That works." She smiled and handed him the cash.

The kid's eyes widened, as if he didn't quite know what to make of her statement. He took the money and counted out change.

"Casey, did my son come in here?"

Allison turned to see the woman she'd been watching a minute ago approach the counter.

The checker shrugged. "No, ma'am, haven't seen him."

"Hmm. That's odd." She ran a hand through her dark hair and sighed. "All right, thank you, hon."

The woman headed back outside, the heels on her cowboy boots clicking on the floor.

"Here you go, ma'am." He handed her the change and set the receipt in the brown paper bag. "Enjoy your time in town while you're here."

"Thanks, Casey, will do." She winked and enjoyed watching the flush creep up the young man's neck.

Grabbing a bag in each hand she opened the door and strode outside into the warm Montana summer air.

She reached Clint's vehicle and had just inserted the key into the lock when she heard heeled footsteps approaching.

"Excuse me."

Allison turned to see the woman from the store rushing her. "Hi." Allison gave her skeptical glance. "Can I help you with something?"

"Yes." The woman stopped in front of her and placed her hands on her hips, narrowing her eyes. "You could tell me what you're doing driving my son's car."

Chapter Fifteen

Allison reared back and just barely avoided flinching. *Well, shit.* She sucked in a quick breath and offered a weak smile. Who would have thought she'd run into Clint's mother? She'd never actually met the woman, since Clint had come out to Seattle by himself during the summers to stay with his grandma.

"Mrs. Novak?"

The woman tilted her head. "You know my name?"

"Of course." She wanted to slap herself for what she was about to say. But the last thing she wanted to do was admit to Clint's mother that he'd kidnapped her. Who would want the responsibility of the hysteria sure to follow? "I'm your son's girlfriend."

The woman blinked and her mouth fell open. She closed it, blinked again then started to say something. Her lips smacked together once more and her gaze turned uncertain.

"Really? You're dating Clint?"

Allison kept her overly bright smile pasted on and gave a quick nod. "Uh huh."

"Oh my goodness." The woman clapped her hands together and squealed. "Well of course you are—and you know, I thought I recognized that sweater of his."

"Yup, it's his." She stuck out her hand. "I'm Allison by the way."

"Allison, so great to meet you." Instead of shaking her hand, the woman stepped forward and threw her arms around her. "And please, call me Lorraine."

"Okay. Lorraine." She gave a weak laugh and returned the hug, patting the taller woman on her back.

"What are you up to?" Lorraine stepped back and eyed the groceries. "Out shopping?"

Relaxing a little, she rolled her eyes. "Yeah. Your son has nothing in the fridge."

"Oh, goodness, I know. I swear that man would gnaw off his own arm before going grocery shopping sometimes."

Allison laughed. "Actually, I could almost believe that. He's home sick right now, so I just popped out for a minute to get him some meds and food."

"He's sick?" Lorraine leaned back, her brows drawing together in a way Allison had seen all too many times on Clint.

"Yeah, nothing big. He just needs to rest."

Allison's stomach clenched as a thought hit her. Oh God. Was his mom going to insist on coming over to take care of him now?

"Oh dear, that's terrible." Lorraine shook her head, her frown deepening. "You must be bored out of your mind, hon. That's it." She gave a fierce nod. "I'm taking you to lunch."

"Oh, I—"

"And I won't take no for answer."

Now it was Allison's turn for to go slack-jawed. When she finally found words, she gave a weak shrug. "But I have ice cream in the bag."

"Oh that's fine. You can stop at his house and drop it off, then we'll be on our way." Lorraine walked around to the passenger side and opened the door. "I'll just leave my car here and we can come back for it later."

Allison, for the second time in minutes, felt her jaw go slack. Was this really happening? Was she about to go to lunch with Clint's mother?

She tugged open the door, tossed the groceries in the back, and slid into the driver's seat. Hopefully her expression didn't look as Twilight Zone as she felt.

"How long have you and Clint been together?"

Yikes. And the questions came rolling.

"Umm, well," she chewed her lip and glanced over her shoulder, backing out of the parking space. "We've know each other since we were kids, I live in Seattle and got to know him when he came out in the summers. But we only recently started...dating. I'm a friend of Kenneth's too."

"Oh. So you and Clint were friends first?" Lorraine sighed. "I love it when that happens. Jack, Clint's dad, and I were friends first. The love part developed over years."

"Really?" Allison glanced over at Clint's mom, who now gazed wistfully out the window.

"Yeah. Well, it really shifted over when Jack got drunk one night after we went to the rodeo." She gave a loud laugh. "He started to strip in the middle of the pasture we were walking in, and told me he was in the mood to do some riding of his own. Namely, me."

Holy mother of God. Allison's eyes widened and her stomach bounced with laughter. If Clint were here right now he'd probably jump out of the vehicle—moving or not.

"Are you and my son intimate?" Lorraine leaned over and patted her arm. "I'm sorry, don't answer that. It's probably better you don't answer. Sometimes I just open my mouth before thinking."

Allison blinked and stepped on the gas. This was just too weird. She wasn't even offended by the question, because truthfully she herself tended to be on the blunt side more often than not.

Still. It was Clint's *mother*.

"Shit."

Allison jerked the wheel at the sudden curse from the other woman.

"I've gone and offended you now, haven't I?" Lorraine sighed. "Sorry. Clint would be pretty upset right now if he could hear me. Especially now that I'm cussing. But I just can't help it when I get all distressed."

Ah, so Clint's mom swore too. Allison laughed and gave the older woman an understanding smile.

"No, you haven't offended me. And I've been known to drop a swear word every now and then myself." She cleared her throat, not ready to admit it tended to be on the more frequent side.

How funny that Clint nagged his mom about the cursing as well.

She pulled the SUV into Clint's driveway and turned off the engine.

"I'll just run in the groceries." Allison glanced over at Lorraine. "Do you want to come in?"

The other woman shook her head and dug into her purse for a powder compact.

"I'd better not, hon," Lorraine prattled nervously as she powdered her face. "If my son finds out I basically abducted you at the store and forced you to lunch, he'll shit a brick."

Allison nodded and slid out of the car, her lips twitching at the abduction comment. Like mother, like son.

She grabbed the groceries from the car and went into the house. It was mostly quiet, save for the faint sound of a television.

She made quick time putting away the food, before hurrying up the spiral staircase to the loft to check on Clint.

Immediately her attention sought out the bed and the figure sprawled out across it.

Clint looked away from the small flat screen on the wall to her. His eyes widened with relief and he made a valiant effort to sit up in bed.

"You're back," he whispered hoarsely.

"I'm back. How've you been?" She strode over to the bed and touched his forehead. "Hmm. Still warm."

He caught her wrist and pressed his cheek into her palm with a groan. "I hurt. Everywhere."

Tingles ran through her arm and down her body, increasing when he pressed a kiss to her flesh.

"Well, that's not good." She stroked the stubble on his cheek and made clucking sound of pity. "How about I get you some more Tylenol and maybe some buttered toast?"

He nodded and moved his cheek against her hand.

"All right. Give me a minute and I'll be right back." She stood up again and rushed back down the stairs.

She glanced at the front door and debated going out to tell Lorraine she'd be a few minutes. Probably no need. If Clint's mom got worried she'd just come inside looking.

Allison heated up some more tea, made some toast with butter, and accompanied it all with Tylenol. There. That oughta hold him over for a bit.

She walked back up the staircase and pursed her lips. Her legs had been getting one helluva workout these past few days. From hiking to the constant stair climbing, not to mention the calf-tightening orgasms.

Clint had turned his focus back to the television, but the minute he realized she'd entered he quickly turned those big *poor me* eyes her way again.

She resisted the urge to giggle at how quickly the big, bold man had turned into a self-pitying, clingy, overgrown boy in need of attention.

She rolled her eyes and set the tray down on the bed. Some men just couldn't handle a bad cold.

He slid his arms around her waist and pulled her onto the bed. His head lowered to her breasts and he groaned.

"Missed you," he muttered.

Okay, maybe he was needy, but her stomach still did butterflies when he clutched her like this. And she had to admit she sort of liked this nurturing thing.

"Did you buy any—" he pulled away and swallowed hard, touching his throat with a wince, "—chicken noodle soup?"

She lifted an eyebrow. "I did, but you'll have to wait for dinner for that luxury. I'm going to lunch."

She stood and went to the mirror on the wall. Wincing at her mediocre appearance, she fluffed her hair. "God, I should've showered this morning."

"Lunch?" he croaked.

She drew in a deep breath and erased the immediate smile that crossed her face.

Turning around she gave a casual shrug, knowing she may have hid the smile, but her eyes still twinkled.

"Yes, lunch. With your mother. She invited me."

The mug full of tea Clint had just lifted clattered back to the tray. His eyes went wide and for a moment all traces of self-pity and sickness seemed to vanish from his face.

"My—"

"Mother. I met her at the store in town." Allison grabbed her purse from the floor. "In fact, I should really get going, Lorraine's waiting in the car."

"*What*?" A look of horror flickered across his face and he tried to climb out of bed.

"No, don't get up. You're sick. This is a girls' lunch," she scoffed and waved him back into bed.

"But—"

"I'll be back in a couple of hours." At the top of the staircase she turned and gave him a quick wink. "Take those pills and maybe try and catch a nap. You'll feel better later. See ya."

She moved quickly down the stairs and out the front door. Not that she actually thought Clint would try to follow—no matter how much he may want to, the guy was still sick.

Lorraine still waited in the car and her gaze lit up when she saw Allison emerge from the house.

Allison opened the door and slid back behind the wheel. "Sorry that took so long. I decided to make him some tea and toast."

"Oh, you're such a nice girl." Lorraine sighed and shook her head. "I don't envy you. I love my son, but I swear when that man gets so much as a cold he reverts to a whiney four-year-old."

Allison started the engine and giggled. "Oh, then it's not just me? I thought for sure he was just pulling that on me because I'm a sucker for it."

"Nope." Lorraine shook her head and winked. "That's the other reason I didn't go inside."

Allison's smile widened as she put the SUV in reverse. Interestingly enough, but she was beginning to think she and Clint's mom would get along just fine.

Where had it all gone wrong? Clint dropped his head back against the pillows and groaned.

It had all seemed perfect this morning. Sure, he was sick and it sucked beyond suckage, but Allison was here. She'd been so sweet and nurturing, so quick to take care of him.

Even while in the throes of this God-awful virus, he'd wanted her. Last night. This morning. And when she'd returned from the store, he'd been ready to convince her to climb into bed with him again. Find a reason to hold her, to touch her.

Oh God, to touch her. The blood stirred in his dick and he groaned. The groan irritated his throat enough to make him start to cough.

The jerky movements of his body knocked the remote control off the bed. It bounced, hitting a button that turned the channel to Lifetime before landing halfway across the room. His eyes widened in horror as a crying woman replaced the baseball game.

Shit. The thought of getting out of bed and walking over to get it made him tired just thinking about it.

And Allison wasn't here anymore to get it for him. He scowled and reached for the tea, now lukewarm.

No, Allie was now out to lunch with his mother. Who in the *hell* would have seen this coming?

He downed the rest of the tea and collapsed back against the pillows—resigned to his fate.

Two hours must have passed before he heard the front door slam again. He was so wrapped up in the show on the television, he barely glanced up when Allison came up the stairs.

"Hey? How are you feeling?" she asked softly, coming over to the bed to sit down beside him.

"Huh?" He jerked his gaze away from the movie and blinked, distracted now.

"Oh my God, are you *crying*?"

He rubbed his eyes and shook his head. "No. No of course not. How was lunch?"

"It was fine." Her brows drew together. "You feel cooler. And your voice doesn't sound as scratch—are you watching Lifetime?"

Heat crawled up his neck as he reached for the tea.

"The remote fell."

She lifted an eyebrow and then looked at the ground. "It's like three feet away."

He offered a stiff shrug and pulled his mind away from the movie he'd unwillingly been sucked into.

She looked relaxed and pretty happy. Obviously lunch had been good. What had they talked about?

Damn. Allison and his mom. What a combo.

"Anyway, lunch was great." She grinned. "Lorraine insisted on treating. She took me to this place that had the most amazing pulled pork sandwiches and potato salad. Mmm."

"Charlie's Ribs and BBQ?"

"*Yes.* That's it. I mean, that shit was good." She slapped her hand against her forehead. "Oh I screwed up already."

"Screwed up?" His brows drew together.

"Yeah. I just swore." She laughed. "Your mom and I made a pact that we'd try and watch our mouths."

His jaw fell slightly. Allison had accomplished what he'd been trying to do for years. He'd always been at his mom to watch her mouth. Kind of the same way he'd been after Allison since they'd met.

"She invited me over for breakfast tomorrow morning. I'm going to do her nails after."

His eyebrows shot up.

Allison laughed. "Don't look so shocked. I used to do nails in a small salon to earn money back when I was in college. And since your mom said she hasn't had a French manicure in years, and the only place that does nails is two hours away, I volunteered. It'll be fun. I don't mind."

Allie used to do nails for a living? Hmm. Actually it kind of made sense. Did this mean Allison would be ditching him again first thing in the morning? A scowl swept over his face. Fortunately he was feeling a bit better.

"Does your throat still hurt?" She leaned forward and cupped his jaw, running her thumbs over his glands. "Hmm. Not as swollen as this morning."

Her soft touch sent a wave of desire through him. His breath hitched.

"I've been drinking tea and sucking cough drops," he said roughly.

"Mmm. Did you miss me?" Her gaze dropped to his mouth. "Or were the women of Lifetime a viable substitute?"

"Shut it," he whispered and crushed his mouth on top of hers.

Her hands slid from his face to the back of his head. He slipped his tongue past the seam of her lips and she made the sweetest little sigh.

She tasted of barbeque sauce and beer, with the hint of woman buried beneath. The taste of Allison he'd grown so addicted to.

He pulled her harder against him, deepening the kiss.

She tore her mouth away and glanced up at him through her lashes. "Yeah. You missed me."

He growled and tugged her T-shirt over her head, making just as quick time unfastening her bra.

Pulling the cotton material from her body, he tossed it to the ground and lifted her pale breasts into his hands.

Her nipples, already hard and now darkened to a berry color, tightened further beneath his gaze.

He met her gaze and ran his thumbs over the tips, watching her drag in a shuddering breath in response.

Lowering his head, he drew one turgid peak between his lips and sucked it deep.

"*Oh.*" She squirmed against him, breathing heavily. "Clint. Wait, hang on."

He scraped his teeth across her nipple, having no intention of calling a halt to the succulent flesh he was enjoying suckling.

"Oh, God. No really. Wait." She pushed at him, panting. "I have an idea."

"It can't be better than this," he argued, burying his face between her breasts and inhaling her scent.

"Well, it's an alternate version of this," she explained. "I couldn't help but notice that pretty fabulous big sunken bath you've got in the bathroom."

He lifted his head. "And?"

"I really want a hot bath," she whispered and trailed a finger down his jaw. "And I really want you in there with me. All that steam will make your throat feel better too."

"Yeah?"

She gave a jerky nod and her tongue darted across her lips. "I was thinking about you all afternoon when I was out to lunch with your mom."

He winced. "Please don't bring up my mother when I'm in the middle of fondling your breasts."

She laughed and her breasts jiggled in his palms, sending more blood straight to his cock.

"Anyway, I've been thinking about it all day," she confessed and pressed her body hard against him. "I just didn't know if you'd be up for it."

"You sure bathe a lot. But I'm up for it," he muttered and released her reluctantly. "Get the bath going, kitten. I'll be in there in a few."

Her eyes widened and she grinned. "Great. You won't regret it."

Watching her hurry across the room, butt jiggling and breasts bouncing, he almost did regret it. Waiting to touch her another few minutes was going to be hell.

He grabbed a condom from his bedside drawer and rolled out of bed, making the slow journey to the bathroom after her.

The ache in his muscles had diminished some from earlier, but in no way had disappeared.

By the time he arrived, the bath was a quarter of the way full and she'd already stripped naked.

"Hey," she glanced over her shoulder as she took one step into the bath.

He slipped his gaze from her luscious body to the floor-to-ceiling windows without curtains behind her. Never before had he thought much about having them in the bathroom. It was on the second floor, with only heavy forest outside. There were no houses or people for miles.

Still, if there *had* been anyone outside they might have gotten a glimpse of Allison's nude body. The realization sent a frisson of possessiveness through him. And hot, thick desire.

"Hurry," she called out, sinking into the tub. "I'm not big on being alone in here."

His response was almost a primitive growl as he stripped off his clothes. Once naked, he stepped into the tub and reached for her again.

Her body, now slick with water, pressed up against him. Her breasts flattened against the hard muscles of his chest, her legs wrapped around his waist.

"I love this room," she murmured. "The view of the trees. How sexy it is to be able to be doing such an intimate act, like bathing, with the whole world to see." She nuzzled his neck. "Only there's no one to see us. You're all alone out here."

"Yes." He agreed and sifted his fingers through her hair, tugging her head back and holding her still. "I like it that way."

"I can see why," she said huskily, her pupils dilating.

He held her hair with one hand and moved the other down her slick back.

Gone was the anger or wariness in her gaze. Before last night, every time he'd touched her it had been a damn battle. Now it was easy. Simple. Natural.

The trust in her gaze surprised him, and the intimacy. When had things shifted? What had sent their dynamic on to a much more fragile and—God, he hated to admit it—terrifyingly intimate level?

"Allison, what the fuck are you doing to me?" he whispered raggedly.

"Hey, now." She pressed a finger to his lips and he couldn't help but notice it shook slightly. "If I'm going to give up swearing then you'd better not pick now to start up."

Her words were light, but he couldn't mistake the sudden vulnerability in her eyes.

He held her gaze, understanding dawned. She was aware of the change too. And maybe just wasn't quite sure what to do with it. How to handle it.

Her breasts lifted against his chest with the deep, uneven breath she took in.

"Clint," she said softly. "Please, touch me."

Chapter Sixteen

The invitation was the needed push to snap him away from his unsettling thoughts.

He reached for the bar of soap, dipped it in the water and then brought it to her breasts. Making slow sudsy circles over the lush swells.

She inhaled sharply and glanced down at her chest. He lowered his gaze as well, watched as her nipples peaked against the white bar.

He dragged it across the tips again and she gasped at the slick friction. Her body arched against him, the legs around his waist tightened.

He cupped water in the palm of his hand, emptying it over her breasts to rinse off the soap. He repeated the process until she was soap free, then moved the bar down over the slight swell of her stomach.

"Oh, Clint..." She sighed and turned her face toward him. Her hair fell in a fan of tendrils, shielding them from the window.

Her lips brushed softly against his, almost hesitant, before growing more confident.

He let her control the kiss for a moment, enjoying the tender exploration. Awareness and pleasure spread through every inch of his body, his cock tightened almost painfully and pressed against the curve of her soft buttocks.

With a growl he slipped the bar of soap lower and pressed it hard between her legs.

He used her gasp of pleasure to slip his tongue boldly into her mouth, taking over the kiss as his control finally broke.

His tongue sought every corner and crevice of her mouth, before coming back to tangle with her tongue.

He continued to rub the soap between her legs, his blood pounding at the fevered whimpers she made. Unable to take it any longer, he abandoned the soap, let it float free as his fingers took over.

Immediately he rubbed the needy little bud before sliding his fingers lower to plunge into her silky, hot heat.

The muscles of her slick channel clenched around him and she emptied a guttural groan into his mouth.

He moved his fingers in and out of her, mimicking the motion of his tongue in her mouth.

Her arms tightened around his neck and she moved against his hand, finally tearing her mouth from his and letting her head fall back on an unrestrained moan.

He lifted her from the water, placing her on the edge of the tub. He went to his knees in the tub and moved between her thighs. Wrapping his hands around her waist, he buried his face between her breasts.

His tongue darted out over the slick flesh, seeking the hardened tips. Allison sighed and delved her fingers into his hair, tugging on the short strands.

He captured one taut peak in his mouth and sucked rhythmically, laving the tip with his tongue.

She squirmed on the edge of the tub, making the sexiest little noises of approval.

He switched his mouth to the other breast, this time using his teeth to gently graze the tight nipple.

"Please," she whimpered. "Oh, God, Clint. I need..."

He tugged on the nipple with his teeth and drew a choked gasp from her.

He released her and stared down at the swollen raspberry tips.

"What do you need?" he demanded, slipping his hand back between her legs and cupping her sex. "Do you need my fingers inside you again? My tongue?"

She nodded, her eyes drifting open. Her eyes, more green now were unfocused and hazy with arousal.

"Please," she pushed at his shoulder, urging him downward. "Your mouth now." Her words were barely audible.

He gave a soft growl of approval and sank back down in the tub. Pushing her thighs apart he draped each leg over his shoulders and gripped her ass, pulling her forward.

He briefly nuzzled the trimmed curls above her mound, before pressing his face into the moist folds of her sex.

He sank his tongue deep into her warm channel and found the musky sweet slickness of her arousal. He lapped it up, his fingers tightening into her soft ass.

Allison cried out and her fingers jerked his hair. Her body pressed harder against his face. He began a slow penetration of her with his tongue, tasting and finding all her desire for him.

His own arousal matched hers and his dick throbbed beneath the water. Each wild cry she emitted sent the blood pounding possessiveness through his veins.

He swept his tongue up from the channel to circle the swollen pearl, knowing her climax was near.

Her hips bucked against him and he tightened his grip on her bottom to keep her still. He drew the bud into his mouth, sucking hard before flicking it quickly with his tongue.

"Oh yes," she cried. "Yes. God. Oh...shi—ooot. Oh. *Oh. God.*"

She screamed and her body jerked, her thighs clenching around his ears.

He licked faster, sucked harder, and when her body started to go limp he pulled her off the edge of the tub.

Sliding his hands to her hips, he urged her legs around his waist, then pushed her hard onto his erection.

He thrust up into her hot tight sheath, still clenching from her orgasm.

His eyes crossed and the air locked in his lungs. He took just a few seconds to savor the feel of her silken heat surrounding his cock, before his fingers bit into her hips and he surged further inside her.

"Ride me," he heard his harsh whisper. "Hard."

Allison's nails dug into his shoulders and she moved on him, lifting herself up and slamming back down. The bouncing motion sent water sloshing over the tub and onto the floor.

With her discovering her own rhythm, he slid his hands up her hips to her ribcage, brushing the undersides of her breasts.

The lush swells bobbed between them and he buried his face between them, licking the nipples and up to the wildly beating pulse in her neck.

"Yes," he ground out. "Kitten, yes."

"Clint." She gasped and moved faster on him. "*Clint.*"

His balls tightened and when she pressed down hard on him, squeezing her muscles around him in her second orgasm he lost it. Emptying himself hard inside her. Again and again. The orgasm ripped through him with an intensity unduplicated, and the urge to cry out he loved her hovered on his tongue, the realization stunning him. A few nights were never going to be enough with Allie. Who had he been kidding?

Only when she collapsed against him, all damp, pliant and warm did he open his eyes and see the unused condom on the far side of the tub.

No wonder it had been so good.

Allison's cheek nuzzled against his shoulder, her breathing uneven.

He closed his eyes again and tightened his arms around her, burying his face in her hair.

She smelled of the eco-friendly shampoo and her perfume—where had she gotten her perfume from? But most of all she smelled like Allison...his woman.

He bit back a groan at the random thought. Like it or not, things had changed.

"We should shower for real now," she murmured against his shoulder, biting him gently and then giggling. "I think we only had time to get me soaped up before..."

They'd screwed like rabbits on steroids. His lips twitched and he eased her off of him.

"You're right. We'll use the actual shower, though."

She slid off him and stood, stepping off the edge of the tub and down the steps onto the rug. He watched her move to the shower stall on the other side of the oversized bathroom and sighed.

He stepped out of the tub as well and scooped up the condom, setting it in a counter drawer. Maybe she hadn't even realized their error. Hell, he barely had. Couldn't make that mistake again though.

"Are you coming?" she glanced out from the stall. "It's my turn to do the soaping, and I've got to tell you. I'm excited."

He laughed and closed the counter drawer, before following her into the shower.

Allison woke the next day in his arms. Sleepy, content, and—if she admitted it—almost completely in love with Clint.

She blinked and stared at his chest. When had it happened? How had it happened?

"Good morning."

She lifted her head, unaware he'd wakened and had been watching her.

"Good morning," she replied, her voice husky. "How are you feeling?"

"About seventy-five percent better." He touched her cheek, the movement gentle and sweet. "Thanks to you, nurse Allie."

She smiled and turned her head to kiss his finger. "It was nothing."

"It was something. You took care of an overgrown whiney man who could barely stumble out of bed. You have a lot of patience. You'll be a great mother some day."

Her stomach twisted and warmth spread to every inch of her body. She watched something flicker in his gaze, like he'd just realized he'd said something he shouldn't have. His expression turned serious before he blinked and it was gone.

"Well," she said lightly and decided to shift the subject. "You certainly recovered your strength by evening."

"Yeah." His lazy smile widened. "I guess I did."

"I'm glad."

His gaze darkened.

"Are you?"

"Yes," she confessed huskily.

His hand slid down to her bottom and squeezed. "What time are you going to breakfast?"

Shoot. She'd almost forgotten. "Nine-thirty. What time is it now?"

His gaze slid beyond her to the clock on the table. "Nine. Bummer."

"Darn. Good thing I showered last night." She drew her bottom lip between her teeth and nibbled, glancing up at him from beneath her lashes. "And I was hoping we'd have time for..."

"Morning sex?"

"Am I that transparent?"

"We both are." He grimaced and adjusted his body.

The brush of his erection against her thigh sent a wave of desire through her.

He cupped her jaw and leaned forward. "How about kissing me good morning, kitten? We at least have time for that."

"At least," she murmured and leaned forward.

She pressed her lips, half parted, against his and lingered for a moment. Taking that second to let the tingles ease down her spine. She brushed her lips across his in a second kiss, softer this time.

After she made the third pass of her lips across his, she slipped her tongue just barely inside his mouth.

He was waiting for her, his tongue moved forward to touch hers gently, before making unhurried strokes against hers.

He traced a finger from her ribcage to her hip, the caress so light that it spread goose bumps over her flesh and sent a tremble rippling through her body.

After a few minutes of the sweet, gentle kiss he finally pulled back.

"Allison," he said quietly, his thumb tracing her mouth. "When you get back today we should talk."

"Talk?" she repeated, still dazed from the kiss.

"Yeah. About us."

"Us." Her heart pounded faster in her chest.

He wanted to talk about them? Did that mean he felt this thing between them? That it was more than two friends who'd decided to try getting sexual? Maybe? Was he thinking of...the future? The idea both terrified her and thrilled her.

"I think that's a good idea." She lowered her gaze, running her tongue over her mouth. "I should probably get ready to meet your mother for breakfast."

"Probably," he agreed with a sigh. "I put your cell phone back in your purse in case you need to reach me."

"Thanks." She slid out of bed and walked over to the duffle bag, grabbing a pair of panties and a bra out. After shimmying into them she went to the closet and slid it open, pulling out the dress she'd hung in there yesterday.

"Where'd you get that?" Clint asked from the bed. "I don't remember buying it."

"You didn't." She gave him a quick grin over his shoulder. "Your mom took me to this most adorable shop yesterday. I couldn't resist and they even carried my perfume. This little town is pretty cool, Clint. I like it."

He lifted an eyebrow, shook his head with a smile. "I can't decide if you're good for each other, or encourage each other's bad habits."

"Probably a little of both." She pulled on the red polka-dot dress. "I love this. It's so retro."

"Yeah...it makes your body look *hot.*" He grinned and climbed out of bed. "Very sexy."

"You sure know how to flatter a girl," she murmured when he stopped in front of her.

"I try." His hands slid to her waist and he lowered his lips to hers, taking her mouth in a harder—much more demanding kiss.

When he lifted his head, she was glad to have his hands holding her up.

"Hurry back, kitten," he commanded raggedly.

Leaving him in the first place was going to be hard enough. She nodded and slipped on the pair of red heels she'd also bought yesterday. Grabbing her purse, she headed for the stairs.

"I'll be back before you know it," she promised and flashed him a quick smile before hurrying out of the house.

"You have the loveliest glow about you today, Allison."

Allison blushed from her roots to her toes and smiled over her omelet up at Clint's mom.

"Do I?" she attempted to say lightly. Good Lord, it was written all over her face. The aura of falling in love. This wasn't good. "I, umm, went to bed early last night. Must be all that extra sleep."

"Must be." Lorraine's lips twitched as she lifted a bite of food to her mouth.

Allison cleared her throat and picked up her coffee. "Thank you for breakfast—it's amazing. I don't think I've ever tried to put steak and Swiss cheese in an omelet before."

"It's good, hmm?" Lorraine gestured with her fork and winked. "A great way to use up leftovers from the night before."

"I'll remember that." She took another bite of omelet and bit back a sigh.

What was Clint doing right now? Probably eating a cold bowl of cereal or something. By himself. Though she was enjoying her breakfast with Lorraine, part of her would have given anything to be back in bed cuddling with Clint.

"I'm so thrilled you're going to do my nails, Allison." Lorraine took the last bite of her toast and pushed her plate aside, folding her arms and looking at her. "I haven't had a decent manicure since I left Portland."

"You used to live in Portland?"

"Yeah, until I came out here for school. That's when I met Clint's dad."

"And you just never went back?" she prodded. "You stayed here?

Lorraine gave another soft nod.

"And you didn't mind giving up life in the city for...Montana on a permanent basis?"

"Not really." Lorraine shrugged. "When you have the opportunity to be with the man you love, where you are doesn't really matter."

Allison's heart sped up and she lowered her gaze. Would she be willing to do the same? Give up everything in Seattle to move out here? Would Clint ask her to? Maybe that's what he wanted to talk about later...

When she lifted her gaze Lorraine was watching her closely with an appraising look.

Allison flushed and drank the last of her coffee. "That's very sweet. And no regrets?"

"I regret that my nails look like shit." Lorraine winced. "Oops. Sorry, haven't been doing too well on that swearing part. In any case, beyond having bad nails, I have no regrets."

"You could always drive to the nearest town with a nail place."

"Too far and gas prices are awful right now." Lorraine shrugged and her smile turned wistful. "It's not really important, Jack loves me. Bad nails or not."

"Well. It's been awhile, but I promise when I finish with you, you'll once again have fabulous nails." Allison pushed her plate back and stood. "Why don't we go in the other room and get to work on making you a goddess."

Clint stood up from the kitchen table and took his empty bowl of Cheerios to the sink.

He lifted his gaze to stare out the window at the forest beyond. It was a bit unsettling. The quietness of the house.

Allison hadn't even been here two days, and yet he'd already grown accustomed to the way she filled his home with laughter and fun. Not to mention sensuality. Things were never dull.

Part of him wondered if maybe he just liked having a woman around—that any would have done. But the notion didn't settle well, made his stomach churn in protest. No. Not just any woman could affect him this way, it was Allie. It'd always been Allie.

He rinsed off his bowl and sighed, rubbing a hand over his bare abdomen. Hell, he was still hungry.

His mouth twisted in a wry smile. Allison had probably eaten some fancy breakfast—his mom loved any opportunity to cook.

Glancing at the clock, he noted it was almost eleven. He should probably get dressed. Walking around with pajama bottoms on wouldn't do if Allie and his mom were to drop by.

The doorbell rang and he froze. Damn. Now how was that for timing? But they wouldn't show up this early, would they?

He dried his hands on the towel hanging from the stove handle and walked slowly back into the living room.

Clint glanced out the window as he moved toward the front door. He grunted as he spotted Pete's, the town Sheriff, car out front. Great. Likely come to tell him there was some kind of mischief going on up in the state park. Wouldn't be the first time.

He grabbed the knob and pulled open the door.

"Morning, Pete. What can I do for you?"

The older man took off his hat and twisted it in his hands, his face reddening. "Ah, hey there, Clint. Look, can I come in? We need to talk."

Unease settled in Clint's gut and he gave a terse nod, opening the door wide and stepping back.

Before Pete could step over the threshold another man came charging in through the open door.

Clint barely had a moment to react before hard palms slammed into his chest, sending him stumbling backwards.

"Where the hell is she?" Ken demanded.

Still a bit weak from being sick, Clint barely caught himself before he could topple over the coffee table. A slow tic started in his jaw as adrenaline sent blood rushing through his veins. He narrowed his eyes at his old friend.

"I told you to wait in the car and I'd handle this," Pete said tersely and tried to pull Ken away.

Ken broke free from the older man's grip and circled Clint again.

"What the hell were you thinking, Clint? Kidnapping Allison?" Ken growled.

"You've got the wrong idea," Clint warned, his voice low and harsh. How the hell had Ken found out? Had Allison's friend turned him in?

"That's what I done told him, Clint." Pete sighed. "The man nearly busted down my door this morning insisting you'd kidnapped someone."

Clint's fists clenched and the air seethed out from between his teeth.

"What the hell are you doing here, Ken? You're getting *married* on Sunday."

Kenneth shook his head. "Yeah, I'm not sure on that anymore. I think I still have feelings for Allison."

"The hell you do," Clint growled, seeing red.

"What's with you?" Ken's gaze ran over him with disgust. "How long have you been planning this? I know you always had a little thing for her, but kidnapping her? Jesus, Clint. Maybe you were always just a little jealous that I got to fuck her first?"

Clint's jaw flexed as he struggled with his temper. "Get out of my house."

Ken stepped forward until they were nose to nose, sending Clint's blood pressure up another notch.

"Where is she?"

"Back the hell off," he growled.

"Did you force yourself on—*oomph.*"

Ken flew backwards from the impact of Clint's fist, tripping over the couch and landing on his side.

"Jesus," Pete whispered. "Clint, you can't just—"

"He's speaking nonsense. I didn't kidnap anyone."

But technically he had. And if Allison had reported it...his stomach churned with bile. After all that had happened between them. Would she have?

Ken stumbled to his feet, eyes wide as he clutched his jaw. "I'm not lying. She told me in her own words."

"Who did?" Pete and Clint demanded at the same time.

"Allison," Ken said with a slow nod. "Allison told me this when she called me. That Clint had kidnapped her."

The tic in Clint's jaw increased. Allison had called Ken? It wasn't possible. It couldn't be. He'd had her phone the entire time. Which meant she would have had to do it when he got sick and they'd returned to his house. *No.* She wouldn't have done that.

Wouldn't she? The seed of doubt had again been planted and his unease tripled. Especially when he remembered her words. *Just because you were the man inside my body, doesn't mean you were the one inside my head.*

"This is bullshit," he muttered, shaking his head.

"Is it?" Ken gave a harsh laugh, then winced, rotating his jaw. "I don't think so. You've gone way too far."

The vision of Allison curled up in his arms this morning swept through him. The trust and softness in her gaze. No. She hadn't had the look of a woman who'd just betrayed him.

Heavy silence filled the room, before Ken bolted for the staircase to the loft above.

Clint thrust a hand through his hair, too confused to even try and stop him.

"What's going on, Clint?" Pete stepped forward and sighed. "He seems dead set that you kidnapped some lady."

"I didn't kidnap her, Pete," he growled. "Not really."

"Not really?" Pete's eyebrows shot up. "Now, Clint—"

"She's here." Ken's footsteps pounded heavily on the wooden stairs. "Or at least she was."

He threw a piece of fabric at Clint's feet. Clint glanced down and recognized the dress Allison had been wearing the day he'd first taken her.

Pete's gaze whipped back to Clint. "Buddy? What's going on?"

"Don't *buddy* him, damn it," Ken snarled. "You should be arresting him. Reading him his rights. Fuck, what the hell is *wrong* with law enforcement in small towns?"

"Who does that dress belong to, Clint?" Pete asked quietly.

Clint's jaw clenched and he exhaled slowly from his nostrils. The shit had just hit the fan. "It's Allison's."

"Why did you take her? To stop her from seeing me? So she couldn't tell me that she wanted me back?" Ken shook his head. "It didn't work. I found out anyway when she called."

Lies. They had to be lies.

"Tell me where she is." Ken got back in his face, then seemed to think better of it, touching his jaw as he scurried backward. "What'd you do with her?"

"You'd better answer the question, Clint," Pete said, sounding a bit weary now.

Clint's head swirled with confusion. Something wasn't right. "She's having breakfast at my mother's house."

"With Lorraine?" Pete perked up. "Well see, we can just call her and straighten this all out."

With a terse nod, Clint crossed the room and grabbed his phone. He dialed his mother's number and forced himself to calm down.

How could he have been so blind? Had she just been playing him? Decided to cozy up to him while she waited for Ken to come in with guns blazing?

Shit. His gut clenched when his mom didn't answer. He disconnected the call and dialed Allie's phone.

"They're not answering their phones right now," he finally muttered, hanging up.

"You piece of shit," Ken growled. "You're stalling. He's done something with her, I tell you."

"I haven't done anything with her, goddamn it," Clint roared, finally losing it. "I told you both where she is."

"Clint," Pete touched his shoulder, his voice calm and resigned. "I think we'd better go down to the station for some further questioning until we can locate Allison."

"Jesus, you can't be serious, Pete." Clint jerked his gaze to his friend. He stiffened at the reluctant determination in the other man's gaze. "I see."

"I'm sorry, buddy."

"Don't be sorry. Arrest his ass," Ken snapped from safely behind Pete.

"I'm not arresting Clint. We're just..."

"It's fine," Clint said flatly. "Let me get some clothes on."

He headed upstairs, fists clenched. This morning he'd been convinced that Allison was likely the love of his life. Now he had to accept the fact she was just more inclined to ruin it.

God he was a fool.

Chapter Seventeen

Allison turned off the hair dryer she was using to dry Lorraine's nails and cocked her head. "Did you hear that?"

"Hear what?" Lorraine asked, grinning down at her new manicure.

"I thought I heard the phone ringing."

"Oh, don't worry about it. Whoever it was will leave a message."

Allison glanced at the clock on the wall and frowned. Hmm. She'd been here a few hours already. It had probably been Clint calling, wondering where she was.

Butterflies fluttered in her belly and her lips curved. The possibilities about what he wanted to discuss later had lingered in her mind all morning.

"Are you in love with him?"

Allison blinked. "Oh I..."

"Sorry. I just did that opening my mouth without thinking thing again." Lorraine held up her hand. "I shouldn't have put you on the spot like that."

Maybe not, but the question was valid. Allison bit her lip and analyzed her heart for the answer. The one she found almost made her drop the brush.

She lifted her gaze from Lorraine's nails and met the other woman's gaze in the mirror. Understanding dawned in Clint's mother's eyes and her mouth curved.

Allison fumbled for words. "I…"

"My nails look great, hon." Lorraine changed the subject and lifted her hands in front of her. "You could have your own shop. You're so good you could do a movie star's nails."

The tension eased from Allison's shoulders and she gave a wry smile. "I'm a teacher now. I used to work in an upscale salon, but I could hardly see myself in Hollywood."

"How about Montana?"

Allison's stomach twisted. The idea actually held appeal and she'd be lying to herself to say she hadn't been considering the possibility all morning. There was something about this town. Its people. The slower pace of life.

"Lorraine—"

A loud knocking on the front door cut off the confession that had been on the tip of her tongue.

"Now I wonder who that could be." Lorraine sighed and pulled herself up from the folding chair. "Let me just check real quick."

"All right. I'll just start cleaning up in here."

Once Lorraine had left the room Allison started collecting the bottles of polish and remover they'd bought yesterday. She'd just put them back into a black makeup bag when she heard the commotion.

She set the bag down and hurried into the front room.

Lorraine stood next to an older lady who looked out of breath and completely distressed.

The woman's gaze turned to her and her jaw dropped. "Is that her?"

"Me?" Allison pressed a hand to her chest and looked behind her. "What?"

"Are you Allison?"

"Last time I checked." Premonition had her gut clenching.

Relief washed over the new woman's face and she strode forward and grasped her arm.

"Come on, you've got to come with me."

Lorraine shook her head. "Rosemary, what the hell is going on?"

"Watch the swearing," Allison reminded her absently.

"Shit. Sorry, I forgot."

"Yes. Please, what *is* going on?" Allison pleaded.

"I'll tell you what's going on." The woman jerked her head toward Lorraine. "My husband just called to tell me that he's going to have to book your son on kidnapping charges."

"Kidnapping charges?"

"*What?*"

Allison and Lorraine both spoke at once.

"But that's impossible," Lorraine sputtered. "Who did he kidnap? And what the hell does Allison have to do with it?"

Allison made no attempt to call her on the curse this time. She'd gone numb and swayed unsteadily on her feet.

"Allison. They're saying he kidnapped Allison."

"Allison?" Lorraine's gaze jerked toward her. "That's ridiculous. Who said such a lie?"

"It's not a lie," Allison blurted before she could stop herself. "I mean, it is. But it isn't. It—*shit.*" She closed her eyes and clenched her fists. "God, who in the hell called the police?"

"Clint kidnapped you?" Lorraine grabbed the back of the couch, her eyes wide and brimming with accusation. "My son? I don't believe it."

"Who called the police?" Allison asked again. Her stomach churning.

This wasn't good. This so wasn't good. Who had called could have possibly—?

"Some guy named Ken showed up and said you'd called him. Said you'd told him you were kidnapped." Rosemary placed her hands on her hips and glanced her over from head to toe.

Lorraine gasped.

"Is it a lie?" Rosemary asked, her gaze still on Allison.

Her mouth opened to deny it but no words came out.

Kenneth. Oh God. That phone call up in the state park. He'd heard her after all. She raced over the conversation in her head that she'd had with him. She hadn't told him to call the police, but he'd obviously decided to do it on his own.

"What have you done?" Lorraine's demanded brokenly.

Allison's gaze moved to Clint's mom and her stomach dropped. Tears brimmed the other woman's eyes and her hands shook.

"You called the police on my *son?*"

"I didn't," Allison protested, but knew she sounded ridiculous to her own ears. She hadn't, but Kenneth had.

"Look, Pete said there's still time. We need to get down to the station right now." Rosemary gave Allison a sharp glance. "Unless you're pressing charges?"

"Of *course* not," Allison cried, horrified. Press charges against the man she'd fallen in love with?

Oh God. This had gone from bad to worse in a matter of seconds.

She drew in an unsteady breath. "Look, take me to the station and we'll get this straightened out."

Rosemary gave a quick nod. "We can take my car. I'll call Pete on the way and let him know we're coming down."

"I'll grab my purse and meet you outside," Lorraine muttered.

Allison hesitated, knowing she ought to try and explain this to Clint's mom.

"Lorraine, I—"

"Not now, Allison." Clint's mother lifted her hand to cut her off, her mouth tight as she avoided looking at her.

Allison fell back, walking slower as Rosemary and Lorraine hurried out the door. A knot lodged in her throat and her stomach felt like she'd just eaten a dozen bricks.

"By the way, Lorraine," Rosemary commented as they climbed into the sedan. "I love your nails."

Lorraine responded with a quiet harrumph and Allison's nausea doubled. She fastened her seatbelt and closed her eyes. Whatever happened next wasn't going to be pretty.

"I don't understand why you haven't been arrested yet," Ken grumbled, pacing the small room.

Clint's jaw clenched and he had the urge to get up from the wall he leaned against, walk over to his old friend and deck him again. When had Ken become such a prick?

But hell, he'd avoided getting read his rights this long, why push his luck.

Pete hung up the phone, ending the call he'd answered a minute ago and glanced up at them.

234

"My wife is bringing your mom and Allison down to the station," Pete said, kicking his legs up on the desk. "And it looks like Allison's not pressing charges. Though of course I'll have to confirm it with her when she arrives."

Clint's head snapped up. She wasn't pressing charges? *Easy there, it doesn't change the fact that she turned you in in the first place.*

"Not pressing charges?" Ken snapped. "I don't believe it. You fucking nature freaks have brainwashed her."

"Watch it there, son," Pete warned, his eyes narrowed. "Or you may find yourself the one getting charged."

Ken's eyes rounded, but fortunately he kept silent.

The women arrived a few minutes later. Rosemary came in first, followed by his mother, who looked pale and concerned, and then Allison walked in.

Allie's body was rigid with tension and her chin was high as she entered the office. Her gaze landed on him for not even a second, before sweeping to Ken.

"*Kenneth?* What in the—?"

"Allison." Ken rushed across the room and pulled her into his arms. "Hon, are you okay? When you called me and told me what had happened I flew out as soon as I could."

Jealously and anger stabbed deep in Clint's gut and his jaw hardened. And there it was, plain and simple, the proof that she'd betrayed him.

Allison snorted. "Ken, when I called—"

"Excuse me, Ms. Donaldson?" Pete cleared his throat.

"What?" She glanced back, annoyance clear on her face.

"I need to verify whether or not you'll be pressing charges against Clint here."

Her gaze widened. "No. I'm not pressing charges. I never meant..."

"Am I free to go?" Clint interrupted, keeping his tone flat, trying to hide any trace of emotion.

The last thing he wanted was for Allison to see how much of a mind fuck this all was to him.

"Uh," Pete hesitated, before nodding. "I guess so, Clint. I'll just need to talk to Ms. Donaldson a bit longer, but if she's not pressing charges, then you're free to go."

"Clint?" Allison's voice cracked through the room as he made his way toward the door. He ignored her and kept striding outside.

"Clint, wait." She followed him out, her feet crunching in the dirt parking lot.

He drew in a ragged breath and turned to face her.

"Hey," she said softly. "Let me just finish up in here and then we'll talk."

"Sorry, kitten." He forced a brief, somewhat callous smile. "That boat's sailed."

"Excuse me?" Her eyes widened, uncertainty flickered in her gaze. "I thought you wanted to...I can explain—"

"Just answer me this. Did you call Ken?"

He watched the guilt flicker in her eyes and her mouth opened and shut a few times. Finally she nodded.

"Yes. I did. But that was—"

"You know, Allie." He folded his arms across his chest and shook his head, looking past her shoulder and at the mountains off in the distance. "You were trying real hard to break up Ken's wedding."

"Maybe I was, but it wasn't—"

"And congratulations. You finally did it. Ken called it off for you."

The sudden silence drew his gaze back to her face. Her jaw had dropped and the shock on her face was blatant.

"Ken called off his wedding?" she whispered. "But..."

"Don't pretend that's not what you wanted the whole time."

"I didn't," she protested. "I mean, yes I didn't want him to marry Ashley, but—"

"Honestly, Allison, I can't really blame you for calling the police. I was an idiot for taking you in the first place. It's just...I've been wanting you for a helluva long time. And when this Ken thing came up I saw it not only as a way to take you out of the equation, but get you out of my system." That part was true. "And it worked." There was the lie.

She continued to stare at him, her face pale now.

"It worked?" she repeated after a moment. "What do you mean by that?"

He gave a harsh laugh, and because he was weak, reached out to run a finger down the soft curve of her jaw one last time.

"It worked," he forced out as casually as he could. "We fucked. It was good. And now we go back to life as normal."

She reared back and slapped his hand away, her body trembling visibly.

"Allison." The door to the station swung open and Ken stood in the doorway. "Come back in here, hon. Let's just get this crap over with so we can get out of this town and back to reality."

"Go back to reality, Allison," Clint taunted, each word cut out a little of his heart. "It's safer there."

"Fuck you."

"You sure didn't stick to that non-swearing goal for long, did you?" he mocked and shook his head. "Thanks for not pressing charges, kitten. I appreciate it."

"Yeah, you'll be lucky if I don't change my mind," she whispered raggedly.

Before he could do something stupid, like beg her to ditch Ken and consider giving up everything to be with him, he turned on his heel and strode across the parking lot.

It didn't matter that he didn't have his car, if he were lucky the three-mile walk home might make his feet hurt. Better than his heart.

"So how are you holding up?" Leah glanced away from the road for a second. "I mean, really."

Allison drew in an unsteady breath and turned to look out at downtown Seattle which they were passing by.

God, talk about the question of the hour. Or week. Make that five weeks, since that's how long it had been since she'd left Montana. Had left Clint.

Her stomach twisted and that recurring lump in her throat once again made an appearance.

"I'm..." Why keep lying? "Fucking awful."

"Oh, gosh, Allison." Leah sighed. "Well at least you're honest. I wish there was something I could do."

"It's not your problem." She stared at the buildings of the city thrusting up into the gray skyline.

"But it is. It is my fault, Allison." Leah groaned. "I made a bad choice that day you called me. If I had told him to bring you home, or threatened to call the police—"

"If you had done either of those things I wouldn't have had that brief, but absolutely wonderful experience with Clint." Her eyes blurred with tears as she remembered his last words to her. *We fucked. It was good. And now we go back to life as normal.*

"Don't blame yourself for what happened, Leah. I screwed everything up the minute I called Ken."

Her stomach churned and she fought another wave of nausea. She pressed her hand against her belly and closed her eyes.

"You look pale, sweetie. Why don't we grab some breakfast."

"I don't want to eat." Allison shook her head. "The very idea makes me wanna ralph."

"Well how about coffee?"

"I don't want you to feel obligated to take care of me. You've already done enough. Really, I'll be all right." Her lips twisted downward. "As they say, nobody ever died from a broken heart."

"Hmm." Leah shook her head. "Let's stop at Ooo La Latté, say hi to Madison, that'll cheer you up."

Leah swerved across three lanes of traffic and exited the freeway.

"What happened with Ken?" Leah asked. "Did he really think you wanted him back?"

Allison snorted and gave her first honest laugh in days. "Yeah. He did. Crazy."

"And he called off his wedding?"

"Yeah. But apparently he did that before I called him. I guess he found Ashley in bed with the FedEx guy." Allison sighed. "Did I call it or what? Apparently both of them are monogamously challenged."

"Yeah, I've always thought he was a bit of a dick." Leah giggled and turned into the parking lot of Ooo La Latté.

"Ken's always been a bit of a playboy. I always thought he had a good heart under it all, but lately, I don't know, he's gotten worse. He's become a bit of a jerk, sadly."

"Allison...have you tried to talk to Clint?"

Every muscle in Allison's body went rigid. Talk to Clint? Right. If only it were that easy. If only that could possibly solve the issue. Tears pricked again behind her eyes but she blinked them away.

"Clint made it pretty clear what kind of relationship we had," she said quietly. "There's really nothing more to talk about."

"I don't know, Allison. I really don't."

"Look, please, I can't talk about this right now." Her voice cracked. "I just *can't*."

"Okay. All right." Leah lifted her hands in surrender and nodded. "Let's go inside and get some coffee."

Allison followed Leah inside and tried to force a small smile on her face. They were regulars here, and she didn't want to get Maddie—the owner of the shop—asking what the hell was wrong with her.

"Allie. Leah." Madison called out in greeting from behind the espresso counter. "How are you?"

"Doing great," Leah replied and cast Allison a quick look. "We both are."

"Right," Allison replied with as much energy as she could muster. "Everything's great."

Madison's gaze narrowed with suspicion as she stared at Allison, and Allison swore beneath her breath. So much for faking it.

"You don't look so hot, Allie. Are you feeling okay?" Madison asked, wiping the counter down with a rag.

"Just fighting a bug. I'm fine." She shifted her gaze and nodded. "Really."

"Hmm. I'm not buying it, but I'll stop pushing." Madison tossed the rag into the sink behind her and sighed. "What can I get you ladies, your usual? Nonfat mocha and an Americano?"

The idea of an Americano had Allison's stomach rolling and she pressed her palm against it.

"Actually, Maddie, I'll just do a tea today. Chamomile if you've got it."

Madison nodded slowly. "We've got it. Sure, no problem. Nonfat mocha for you, Leah?"

"Sounds perfect. Thanks, Maddie. Hey, how's that little girl of yours?"

"Turned eight months last week," Madison grinned as she went to make their drinks. "Crawling all over the place."

Eight months? Allison bit back a sigh. It seemed like just yesterday Madison announced she was pregnant. God, time flew. Seeing the glow of happiness on the shop owner's face sent a pang of jealousy through Allison's gut.

Everyone seemed happy. Everyone had found the love of their lives and seemed to live happily ever after. *Everyone but me.* No, the man she loved wanted nothing to do with her anymore.

Feeling the sting of tears in her eyes, she bit back a curse at her weakness and cleared her throat.

"I'm not feeling well," she muttered to Leah. "If you don't mind, I'll just go sit down on one of the couches."

Leah nodded, her brows drawn together in concern. "Of course. Go sit down."

Allison walked over to a big leather couch and sank down, lowering her head into her hands. She should have never let Leah talk her into going out this morning.

All she'd wanted was to stay in bed and cry—then cry some more. But then she'd done that just about every morning since she'd left Montana, so she could kind of understand Leah's determination to get her out of bed.

"Here's your tea."

Allison hurried to brush away a lone tear, but she didn't delude herself into thinking Leah hadn't seen it.

She lifted her head and gave a wan smile, taking the tea from her.

"Thank you."

"You're welcome. And Maddie insisted on giving you a muffin. She says you're too skinny. Nibble on it. You need something in your stomach."

"You guys are such tyrants," Allison grumbled but took the muffin as well.

"Only when we need to be." Leah grinned, then cleared her throat. "Can I borrow your phone for a minute?"

"My phone?" Allison reached into her purse for her cell. "What happened to yours?"

"I left it on my bedside table. Can you believe it?"

Allison set her phone in Leah's palm and took a sip of tea. She watched as her friend disappeared outside and sighed.

With the tea warming her belly now, she closed her eyes briefly. She'd always assumed she'd be a city girl for life...until Montana had started to look mighty appealing.

Her stomach churned again and she set the muffin down on her lap before she could even think of taking a bite.

Ugh. Something had to give. Because this whole depressed as hell thing just wasn't working for her.

She took another sip of tea and blinked away a fresh wave of tears.

Chapter Eighteen

Clint had just grabbed his keys off the desk in the front room when the phone started to ring.

He glanced at it and scowled. It was likely just his mother calling again to remind him what a fool he was.

The minute he'd confessed that he had indeed kidnapped Allison, and that she'd been telling the truth, his mother hadn't let him hear the end of it. She wanted him to go after Allison and get her back.

If only it were that simple. Hell, if he thought he stood one iota of a chance with her, he'd be on the first plane over to Seattle. But he wasn't that delusional. By now Allison was probably well on her way into her second attempt at a relationship with Ken.

Bitterness ate at his gut and he pushed aside the ache in his heart. He needed to forget her. Move on. Ask out Barbara Feldman who'd just gotten a divorce. She was pretty, respectable, friendly—*and not Allie.*

The phone stopped ringing and he sighed, wondering if they'd just leave a message. The thought barely crossed his mind before it started ringing again.

"Jesus, Mom." He strode across the room and lifted the receiver and bit out a sharp, "Hello?"

"Is this Clint?"

His brows drew together at the slightly familiar feminine voice.

"Yes. Who's speaking?"

"You're an asshole."

Clint blinked in dismay. "Who is this?"

"Leah," she said, sounding seriously peeved. "I'm Allison's friend, remember?"

His blood quickened and he tightened his grip around the receiver. Allison's friend was calling him. Why? How?

"I got your number from Allison's phone," she went on as if knowing his thoughts. "I just figured I should call and point out what a piece of shit you are."

"You have the same foul mouth as her," he muttered and before he could stop himself asked, "How is she?"

"I don't swear that much, really, but you're bringing it out in me." She sniffed. "And why do you care how she is? She was just some random sex to you, right?"

"Don't put words into my mouth."

"I'm not putting them there, you put them there."

"Look—"

"Do you know she's been crying for over a month now?"

His muscles went rigid, his chest tightened. "Excuse me?"

"She doesn't eat. Is just this pale and weak shell of her normal self."

"What's wrong with her?" he asked sharply. God, Allison would likely beat her friend to bits if she knew all the things Leah was telling him.

"What do you *think* is wrong with her?"

"What the hell kind of mind game are you playing?" he exploded. "Has Ken taken her to the doctor?"

"*Ken*? What does Ken have to do with anything?"

Clint drew in a slow breath, though it was more difficult. "They're together." He paused and could barely get out the next question. "Aren't they?"

There was a long silence on the other end of the phone and the faintest bit of hope sparked in his heart. Then Leah burst out laughing.

"Oh God. Talk about five weeks wasted. Did either of you even *try* to talk things through?"

"Leah, answer the damn question," he snapped through gritted teeth, his heart pounding furiously in his chest now. "Is she with Ken?"

"You know what I'm going to do? I'm going to remind you of Allison's address. You show up there tonight and try having a real conversation."

"You want me to fly to Seattle to get an answer?" he snapped in disbelief.

"Clint," her voice quieted, turned serious. "Trust me. It'll be worth your while."

His pulse slowed, before speeding back up, the hope in his chest expanding.

"I'll be on the first flight out."

Allison slipped out of her jeans and climbed into bed wearing only a T-shirt and bikini panties.

She flipped on the easy listening station, grabbed her book off the nightstand, and pulled the comforter up to her chin.

Alone at last. Finally. Leah had been surprisingly easy to push out the door, despite her friend's earlier protests that

Allison really ought to get out and do something on a Friday night.

But she didn't want to do anything. She wanted to stay in bed and hide from the world. At least until she woke up one morning and discovered she was no longer in love with a man who didn't love her back.

She sniffled again and glanced at the box of tissues on the other side of the room. Shoot she knew she'd forgotten something.

Flipping open the book, she tried to read, but the words were just a blur in front of her unfocused gaze.

After an hour she was about to finally turn a page in the book when the doorbell rang.

She gave a growl of frustration and threw the book at the wall.

Why couldn't Leah just back off? Being around people right now sounded about as fun as having teeth pulled without Novocain.

Shoving the comforter back, she swung her legs out of bed, then headed for the front room. She didn't stop to grab a robe—her friend had seen her walk around without pants on before—just marched straight to the front door and swung it open with a snarl.

"Look, I said—oh my God." She slammed the door closed, her pulse doubling to a mile a minute.

He was here. Oh God. Clint was here, standing on her doorstep. And she'd just slammed the door in his face.

The doorbell rang. Again. And again as he held down the button. Christ, her neighbors were going to complain.

She twisted the handle and started to open the door. She hadn't even cracked it an inch before he pressed his palm against the wood and pushed it all the way open, striding into her apartment.

"Do you mind?" She hurriedly shut the door before her neighbors could see her standing half naked in the doorway. "I didn't invite you in."

"I didn't ask for an invitation." His gaze drifted around her apartment before moving back to her, lingering on her swollen eyes and red nose. "You look like hell."

She issued a choked gasp in outrage. "You...damn it that was rude."

His lips quirked as he made a lazy inspection from the top of her head to her bare toes, which she curled into the carpet. His gaze lingered longest on her tiny yellow panties. Damn it. She should've put on the robe.

He was so tall his presence seemed to engulf the entire apartment. Or maybe it was just how aware of him she was.

She folded her arms across her chest. Her heart pounded so fast she was sure her left breast would start bouncing.

"Actually, you kind of do need an invitation into my apartment. Otherwise it's called unlawful entry or something along those lines. I could call the police..." She drifted off, her bravado slipping as heat stole into her cheeks.

So the wrong thing to say, and she knew exactly what his next comment would be.

"You've already done it once, I wouldn't be surprised." He took a step toward her and she hastily retreated backward.

"I didn't call the police on you," she muttered and kept moving away from him, but he continued to follow.

Her hips bumped into the back of her couch and he used the object to corner her. His arms settled on each side of her hips, curling around the edge of the couch.

His body was so close to hers that her breasts brushed against his chest. The familiar smell of him—the outdoors and soap, filled her senses. Dizzying her.

"Didn't you?" he lifted an eyebrow.

She shook her head stupidly, her tongue glued to the roof of her mouth. What was the question?

"You told Ken to though."

She shook her head again in denial, but still found it impossible to actually form words.

He lifted one hand to cup her jaw and his thumb brushed across her lower lip.

Tingles rocked through her body and her nipples tightened against his chest. Oh God. She wanted him so badly it hurt. As much today as five weeks ago.

Clint's gaze dropped between them to where her breasts rose and fell with each jerky breath she drew in.

"Clint," she finally asked raggedly. "Why are you here?"

"You know why." His thumb swept over her lip again. His head lowered, before his mouth covered hers.

Heat ignited in her body, raced through every nerve ending. She knew she should push him away—demand he get out of her apartment and out of her life.

But knowing and doing it were completely different things. Her body and heart wanted him in a way that was completely irrational and foolish. And it didn't matter. Any of it.

One more time. Just one more time.

She gave a groan of surrender and wrapped her arms around his neck, opening her mouth to the slick invasion of his tongue.

The kiss turned hard and desperate, each sweep of his tongue against hers added another layer to the sharp intensity of her desire.

Her sex ached and grew heavy, moisture gathered in her panties. She moved her legs apart and he stepped between them, his thighs urging hers to part further.

He moved a hand between them to cup her through her panties and she whimpered.

"God, I've missed you," he whispered raggedly, his fingers worked beneath the thin lace, before pushing past her swollen folds and into the heart of her.

Allison cried out, moving against his hand. He lowered his gaze to where his fingers moved in and out of her channel. She clutched his forearms, her head falling back as pleasure spiraled inside her. Higher. And faster. Until the world around her exploded into a mass of color and sensation.

She was dimly aware of him pulling his fingers from her and adjusting her panties again.

"Sexy little kitten," he murmured, kissing her neck. "You drive me mad watching you come."

Allison swallowed hard and shook her head. "Clint, I—"

"I want you, Allie. But we need to talk. And before that, let's get us a shower first," he suggested quietly.

She blinked. "A shower?"

"Did you miss that part where I said you looked like hell?"

Her nostrils flared and resentment swept through her. "Say that again and I swear I'll kick you in balls. And what do we need to talk about?"

Anger flickered in his gaze before it was snuffed out and replaced with indifference.

"Shower first, Allie."

She wanted to scowl, or give some flippant reply, but she was too tired. Physically and mentally.

With a terse nod she made her way to the bathroom and turned on the shower.

Stripping naked, she climbed under the warm spray of water. A moment later Clint climbed in with her.

She stepped to the corner of the stall, her pulse spiking. Even with the intimate moment they'd just shared, she still didn't trust him. Or his intentions. And he still hadn't answered why he'd shown up at her apartment.

"Come here."

She jerked at his soft command, but closed the distance between them.

He brought the bar of soap over her body. His touch was surprisingly tender as he washed her from head to toe.

When he reached for the shampoo she wasn't even surprised anymore, just closed her eyes and let him lather up her hair.

Five minutes later he turned off the shower and ushered her out, wrapping her in a big fluffy towel.

Even if a little strange, it seemed all too comfortable to have Clint take care of her like this. Too sweet.

"Hang on a second," he murmured and left the bathroom.

She walked to the mirror and looked at her image. Some of the color had come back into her face—her cheeks definitely had more pink in them.

"Okay."

Clint's image appeared in the mirror and she turned around.

"Here, I want you to take this."

She lowered her gaze to the object in his hand her eyes widened.

"What?" She jerked her gaze back to his face, her mouth gaping. "Clint—"

"Take it." He pushed the pregnancy test into her hand. "I'll wait in the other room while you do."

She stared at him, aghast. He thought she was pregnant?

"This is ridiculous."

"Take the damn test, Allie." He stepped forward, irritation flickering in his eyes. "Or I'll stay in here and make sure you do."

"Oh get the hell out," she snapped and pushed him backward. "You've obviously been reading way too many secret baby books."

She locked the door behind him and glared at the test, before pulling the materials from the box and glanced at the instructions. A minute later she'd started the process and stared at the wand.

"Sorry to disappoint you, but we used condoms in Montana," she called out.

"Not every time."

His quiet response sent a wave of tension through her and the breath locked in her throat. What was he talking about? When hadn't they—

"That night in the bath."

Her mind raced back to that sensual moment they'd had. Probed each intimate detail. Her stomach rolled. Nowhere in her memory could she recall a condom.

The blood rushed to her head and she grabbed the sink. Her whole world rocked on its axis. Oh dear God. The morning nausea. Skipping breakfast all the time and still feeling bloated.

The way her breasts had felt extra achy before she'd gotten her period.

Only she hadn't gotten her period. She'd convinced herself she was just a couple of days late. *Or weeks.* God, she'd lost all track of time.

Allison pressed her fist against her mouth and slid to the floor. She didn't want to look at the wand, which would clearly show the result by now. She didn't even need to. She already knew exactly what the answer would be.

And then what? What would Clint do? Besides make all kinds of claims on her child. Oh God. Their child. The beginnings of hysteria bubbled in her chest.

She stood and grabbed the wand, trying not to acknowledge the plus sign glaring at her as she stuffed it to the bottom of her waste bin.

"It's negative," she blurted, panicking.

There was silence outside the door.

"You can just show yourself out, Clint. Really, there's no need to talk about anything." Her voice cracked. "Everything's just fine. It was a big old negative sign."

"Open the door, Allison," he coaxed softly.

And now she'd blown it. She should've just kept her mouth shut.

"No," she whispered.

"Open the door, Allie."

Tears pricked behind her eyes and she unlocked the door and then pulled it open.

She made no effort to stop him as Clint moved past her to the garbage can to retrieve the wand. It'd be kind of hard to keep a pregnancy a secret anyway.

Allison stepped out of the bathroom and walked into the kitchen. She went to pour herself a glass of water and found her hands shaking enough that she could barely hold the glass.

"Here let me." Clint came behind her and took the glass from her hand, filling it with water.

She accepted the glass from him and wrapped both hands around it to take a sip.

Keeping her gaze lowered, she waited for his anger. For him to ask why she'd lied about the test.

When he didn't say anything, just remained quiet next to her, she lifted her head and gave him a hard look, deciding to make a preemptive attack.

"If you knew we'd forgotten a condom, how come you didn't say anything the morning after it happened?"

His gaze narrowed. "I had planned on it. Before you left to have breakfast with my mother that morning I'd mentioned we needed to talk when you returned." He paused. "Nearly getting arrested changed plans."

The disappointment almost crushed her. Her chest squeezed tight and it became hard to breathe. For so long she'd harbored the fantasy that *the talk* would be for him to confess that he'd fallen in love with her. Maybe wanted her to consider moving to Montana.

Her mouth twisted with regret. But no. He'd only wanted to have the *what if I knocked you up* discussion.

"Okay." She blinked her watery eyes and gave a blasé shrug. "Why did you show up now? Over a month since I'd left?"

"Because Leah called me."

"*What?*" Her vision blurred and her jaw went rigid.

"Apparently she found it necessary to declare how much of an asshole I am—"

"You *are* an asshole," she snapped. "And so is she. I can't believe she called you."

"She cares about you and was worried."

How had Leah even gotten Clint's number? She frowned and took another sip of water. This morning at Maddie's coffee shop...

Her gaze jerked back up.

"She called you this morning?"

"Yes."

"And you drove right over?" her voice sharpened in disbelief.

"I flew."

"But why?" she sputtered.

"Because *I* care about you."

She backed up, her eyes wide and her stomach churning violently. "Don't," she choked out, "even try and tell me such absolute bullshit."

"It's not bullshit."

"It *is*. The only reason you're here—that you're saying any of this is because you knew it was possible that you'd gotten me pregnant," she accused. "I was no better than that virus you had last month, you basically said so yourself. Just something you needed to get out of your system."

"Don't tell me you actually believed me." He followed her as she tried to leave the room, catching her arm and swinging her around. "Because it was all a lie."

She glared at him, her eyes brimming again. "Oh really? And why in the hell would you lie?"

"Self deprivation. What should I have done?" he demanded, his voice rising and anger flickering in his gaze. "You were standing there next to Ken, on the brink of having me arrested. What should I have done, Allison?" he asked again. "Confessed that I'd fallen in love with you?"

Her breath caught, the blood rushing in her ears. He loved her? Her heart swelled with emotion and tears stung her eyes, but she blinked them away.

"It was hard enough to accept that you'd called Ken after that night we spent together at my house." He shook his head, the anguish in his gaze evident. "But I don't care anymore. About any of it. I'm here to beg you to give us a chance. Maybe you don't love me now, but give it time—"

"Wait. Wait, wait, wait. You love me? Oh, hold on, don't answer that yet." She held up her hand. Her mind swirling with everything he was saying, but focusing on one point in particular. "I called Ken from inside the state park. Before we ever went back to your place. That was when I was still really mad at you."

His brows drew together. "I don't understand. How could you have? You didn't have your phone. And, yes, I love you."

"God, I told you not to answer that part yet." She shook her head trying to clear it from the muddle of thoughts. *He loved her.* "I used your phone, but I never asked Ken to call the police. That was his doing." She met his gaze again. "Did you honestly think I would have turned you in after that night we spent together in your house?"

Uncertainty flickered in his eyes. "I didn't want to think it. But, yes, I did." He pulled her against him and cupped her face.

He loved her.

"Were you *ever* trying to get Ken back?"

"No. Never. I just wanted to keep him from marrying Ashley. We went to high school together. She used to tell me how easy it would be to fake a pregnancy and trap a guy into marriage. I was worried that's what had happened to Ken."

"Oh, kitten. God, I'm sorry." He kissed her forehead. "Am I completely out of line to think we might have a chance?"

"No."

He pulled back.

"I mean, no you're not out of line. We do have a chance." She licked her lips again. "But I don't get it. You can't possibly love me, Clint. I'm grouchy at times. I swear too much—"

"Are you trying to talk me out of it?"

"I'm just saying..."

"Stop. It's not going to work." His lips brushed hers. "I love you."

She sighed, relief washing through her as her body weakened against his. She nuzzled his chest and whispered, "I love you too."

"Oh God." He drew in a ragged breath and pulled her into his arms. "Have you ever considered moving to Montana? Getting away from the city? I'm sure they're hiring teachers, or maybe you could open a nail salon. Hell, I don't care what you do, kitten, so long as you're there."

"I've thought about it at least once a day since you dragged me out there," she admitted. "I love Seattle, but I know I'll grow to love Montana just as much. I already started to fall in love with the place when you took me camping. It's beautiful."

"And what about marriage?"

"Marriage?" Her heart clenched and her knees went weak. "Are you...are you asking?"

"Most definitely." He kissed her again. Harder this time. "Are you accepting?"

Oh, God, oh, God. "Most definitely."

Clint swept her up into his arms. "Where's your bedroom."

"Back of the apartment on the right." She snuggled against him, burying her head against his chest.

Her heart swelled with happiness, the knowledge that he loved her clicking on the light inside her again. Offering such relief and peace. Her throat tightened with the love she felt for him. For Clint. Who would have ever known that this was their destiny?

He entered her room and carried her toward her bed, stumbling over something in the process.

His gaze dropped to the book on the ground and he grinned. "And you accused me of reading the secret baby books?"

"It was a gift," she muttered, heat stealing into her cheeks.

"I'm sure."

He set her on the top of her pink comforter and then lay down next to her. "How are you really feeling about this baby thing?"

She hesitated, her hand drifting over her belly. "I'm shocked. Terrified," she admitted. There was a baby in there. Clint's baby. "But...I kind of like the idea of a baby. I can handle it."

"We can."

We. She loved the sound of that.

He kissed her neck, making all her thoughts and worries scatter and a warm, comforting desire take its place.

"But, Allie?"

"Yes." She eased her fingers into his hair, tugging his head down to hers.

God, she loved this man. So much it hurt to think how close they'd come to not being together. Thank God for Leah.

"We do need to work on that swearing thing," he chided. "Unless you want our kid's first word to be asshole."

She grinned, before laughing huskily. "Could be worse. Could be fuck."

"*Allison.*"

"I'll work on it," she promised and pulled his mouth down to hers.

About the Author

Shelli is a New York Times Bestselling Author who read her first romance novel when she snatched it off her mother's bookshelf at the age of eleven. One taste and she was forever hooked. It wasn't until many years later that she decided to pursue writing stories of her own. By then she acknowledged the voices in her head didn't make her crazy, they made her a writer.

Shelli currently lives in the Pacific Northwest with her daughter. She writes various genres of romance, is a compulsive volunteer, and has been known to spontaneously burst into song.

You can visit Shelli at www.shellistevens.com.

One man wants her heart. The other wants her dead...

Going Down
© 2010 Shelli Stevens
Holding Out for a Hero, Book 1

Eleanor Owen needs to get out of Chicago and quick. It's not that she doesn't want to obey the subpoena to testify against her drug-trafficking ex-boyfriend. It's making it to the witness stand alive, should a dirty cop make good on his threats.

Tiny, remote Wyattville, Oregon, looks like the perfect place to disappear, but it's hard to blend into the woodwork when one of the town's infamous namesakes sends her heart racing. Worse, Mr. Tall, Hot and Packing is the town sheriff, which means she should stay as far away from him as possible.

Tyson Wyatt is positive the sexy new girl in town is hiding something. Question is, what? He vows to feel out her secrets—including what she feels like beneath him. Preferably naked. Until then, he's not buying the story she's selling.

Their chemistry is sheet-melting hot, and Ellie realizes much too late that the man with the badge is as dangerous to her heart as her ex is to her life...

Warning: A city girl on the run, and a small-town sheriff set to seduce. Explicit sex. Dirty talk. A hint of danger. Oral sex with a cupcake.

Available now in ebook from Samhain Publishing.

You can always come home. Second chances come a little harder.

A Forever Kind of Love
© 2011 Shiloh Walker

Chase and Zoe were the high school golden couple. Football captain, cheerleader, prom royalty. After graduation, though, Chase couldn't resist the urge to experience life outside their small town. He didn't exactly expect Zoe to wait twelve years for him, but now that he's back, he finds some small part of him hoping she did.

It's no big surprise she's married. The kick in the face is she married his best friend.

Zoe was devastated when Chase left, but she's filed those bittersweet memories under "Moved On". She loves her life, and loves her husband. She has all she needs. And Chase keeps an honorable distance.

One cold, wet, miserable day, tragedy turns Zoe's world upside down. Chase never expected her to simply fall into his arms, but a man can dream. Except his dream doesn't include the fact that this time, she's the one hitting the road...and he's the one left behind.

Warning: This story contains heartbreak, heartache and one last chance for two lovers to find each other.

Available now in ebook from Samhain Publishing.

SAMHAIN
PUBLISHING

It's all about the story...

Romance

HORROR

Retro
ROMANCE

www.samhainpublishing.com

CPSIA information can be obtained at www.ICGtesting.com
Printed in the USA
BVOW041152210512

290724BV00001B/15/P

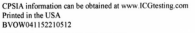

9 781609 286101